LOOTALOOT

LOOTALOOT

BABURAO BAGUL

Translated by
MANAV KAMBLI

hachette
INDIA

Originally published in Marathi in 1969 as मरण स्वस्त होत आहे
First published in English in 2024 by Hachette India
(Registered name: Hachette Book Publishing India Pvt. Ltd)
An Hachette UK company
www.hachetteindia.com

1

ISBN 978-93-5731-773-3

Hachette Book Publishing India Pvt. Ltd
4th & 5th Floors, Corporate Centre
Plot No. 94, Sector 44, Gurugram – 122003, India

Typeset in Bembo Std 11/15.5
by Manmohan Kumar, Delhi

FSC
www.fsc.org
MIX
Paper | Supporting responsible forestry
FSC® C010615

Printed and bound in India
by Thomson Press India Ltd.

To the great Martin Luther King,
You fought
To liberate humankind
And to make them greater
Than they are.
For that,
I reverently dedicate this to you.

Contents

Translator's Note

There is a curious dearth of English translations of Marathi literature. I feel like this is something every regional language translator in India might say for their respective languages, even though the landscape for translations is changing – dare I say, for the better? Of course, there are several reasons for this. One of the most prominent ones is the Booker Prize–winning translation of Geetanjali Shree's *Tomb of Sand* by Daisy Rockwell. Prominent Indian awards, such as the JCB Prize, have also given some brilliant translations their due. However, certain languages have benefitted more than others; Marathi is yet to break into the mainstream in the same way as Hindi or Bengali. This work is a small attempt to bring that treasure trove to a larger audience. The night sky of Marathi literature is littered with breathtaking constellations that merit discovery, discussion and response.

Marathi literature entered my world in tiny bits, like intermittent rain seeping through the interstices of patchy rooftops. A small trickle every now and then, but nothing consistent. My understanding was painfully limited. My discovery of Baburao Bagul's work was a potent mixture of chance and circumstance.

Born in 1930, in Maharashtra's Nashik, Baburao Bagul was sent to Mumbai at the age of ten to live with his aunt. Much of his growth and development happened in the environs of the Matunga Labour Camp, which happened to be a node for the Ambedkarite and other workers' movements, and where Bagul discovered Dalit-Marxist writers such as Anna Bhau Sathe. Bagul's language is clearly impacted by both: the political and the literary forces that swirled in his immediate environment. These influences are catalysed into the pure, creative force that is Bagul's work. Right from his first seminal collection, *Jevha Mi Jaat Chorli Hoti* (When I hid my caste, 1963), we can see his efforts to truthfully and unabashedly capture Dalit realities.

But it was this collection – *Maran Swasta Hot Aahe* (Death is becoming cheap, 1969) – that firmly placed him amidst the most prolific, impactful Dalit voices of his generation. Bagul's craft had been honed considerably, and he takes us viscerally close to the lives of those who society has rendered invisible, inert and mute. His imperfect protagonists trudge through a world where all odds are stacked against them, and the reader is assailed by the feeling of helplessness that the characters experience.

Dalit literature has arisen from cultural conflict. Dalit writers rightly challenge the canonical ideas of 'Hindu literature' and its hegemony. Baburao Bagul reiterates, 'The established literature of India is Hindu literature. But it is Dalit literature which has the revolutionary power to accept new science and technology and bring about a total transformation. "Dalit" is the name of total revolution; it is revolution incarnate'. (Bagul, 'Dalit literature is but human literature,' *Poisoned Bread*, 1992, p. 289.)

Knowing this context is important to understand why Bagul's work is not easy to translate. The act of translation itself, when applied to Dalit literature, becomes far more than just recoding, or bringing certain works to light that need attention in the artistic sense. Brahminical hegemony earlier assumed Dalit writing to be coarse, shallow, crude and without intellectual merit. After all, this writing did not adhere to the mores of 'pure' Marathi, or Praman Bhasha. But Bagul threw these sensibilities back in the face of the hegemon. In an essay in the Diwali issue of *Marathwada* from 1969, Bagul declares, 'Dalit literature believes that looking for the meaning of life in social debates, philosophy or political manifestoes would make it monochromatic. The meaning of life is to be found in Nature.'

So, what can we say about this collection? *Maran Swasta Hot Aahe* is considered to be a milestone for both: Bagul's writing and Marathi literature at large. For one, it definitely provided a stark contrast to Brahminical works and depictions.

The book shook me. The first layer of my reactions was rooted in the content of the stories themselves – Bagul articulated the bitter, abysmal realities of Dalithood in a raw, unfettered form that shredded my sanitized ideas of Marathi narratives. The second layer was simply an appreciation of his craft: the entire collection was remarkable. Each story was different, and the numerous shades of Dalithood were cocooned in the rich, experimental tapestry of Bagul's words. Some stories were sombre from beginning to end; others exploded with barely repressed rage, and then there were those that read like cinematic masterpieces, with an entire range of emotions condensed into a single paragraph.

In this, Bagul's writing was a reflection of the advent of protest culture and Dalit intellectual tradition giving a new outlet to Dalit emotions that had been suppressed, regulated and quelled for centuries. Bagul deftly adopts a stream of consciousness style to do so, giving us access to the character's physical as well as mental discomfort, from the pain shooting through their limbs as they stand under the hot sun, hoping to earn their first morsel of food, to the mixture of rage, frustration and futility in the face of repeated injustices. Yet, there is also a significant difference in Bagul's stream of consciousness, perhaps due to his familiarity with Buddhist thought. Often it's not the protagonist themselves but *their mind* which feels emotions or comes up with a thought. For example: *What if my mind, which loathed him to the core, suddenly had some untoward ideas?* ('Education')

Even though the stories appear to be focused on individuals, Bagul uses them to critique society and bring out the irony in its stereotypes. Thus the notion of an 'educated man' is shattered as we see a well-read, artistic young boy forced to become a gangster to protect his family, even as his privileged classmate enthusiastically participates in the socialist struggle ('Education'); the intense physical and emotional distress faced by what seems to be a group of petty conmen and loafers ('Hard Labour'); and a gang leader risking his life and fighting his own men to prevent a prostitute from being raped ('Goon').

Even as each story depicts harrowing experiences underscored by unending misery, underneath it all simmers the will to power, to rebellion, silent and futile as it may seem, and to decisive revolution.

The shadow of caste haunts Bagul's protagonists incessantly. While other authors dealt with caste and its manifestations in the village space, *Lootaloot* mainly takes us through the labyrinthine slums of Mumbai, as well as the intersections of that space with 'civilization' as we know it. This also adds to the complexity of dialect, since Mumbai as a city, has a profound impact on how characters speak in his stories. Shanta Gokhale, in her foreword to *When I Hid My Caste,* remarked that Bagul's use of dialect also encouraged other emerging Dalit writers to use their own language to powerfully draw on their own experiences.

Baburao Bagul was an excellent orator, and his mastery of dialogue reflects this. His speeches were provocative as he didn't simply attack Hindu supremacy with generic, milquetoast expressions. He focused obsessively on the primacy of nature, science and logic over religious institutions, and Manu – of the infamous *Manusmriti* – was often a target of his ire. Getting to the root cause of our casteist reality and attacking a system that was brushed off as a misunderstood relic of the past that somehow doesn't exist in our newly developed, urbanized realities was his forte.

He also introduces critique that other authors might overlook by depicting Dalit characters who have been shown the 'Brahmanical dream' – i.e., those who are embarrassed of their heritage and aspire to become the shining beacons of modern civilization, while ignoring caste at their peril. From the teacher in 'The Birth of a Poem' to the eloquent Doctor Bapu in 'Thirst', these characters clash with those who have experienced systemic cruelty like none other and evolve. Despite the repeated use of the words *helpless, futile* or otherwise, these characters are drawn to revolt, rebellion and decisive revolution to better their lot by hook or by crook.

I'll end with a note on the book itself so that you can dive into the stories without further ado: Our definitions of death, destitution, suffering and even Hell are varied and often based on personal experience. With *Lootaloot*, Baburao Bagul challenges sheltered sensibilities by penning an open, bare-faced collection of short stories that force us to be objective. Objective in our understanding of what suffering really *is* – or at least *can* be. But beyond these personal readings lies the politics of Dalit writing and, ultimately, the unapologetic depiction of Dalithood as a lived, persistent experience. I hope this translation can continue the legacy of Baburao Bagul's work. Read, reflect and respond to this text in the ways you sincerely see fit.

लुटालूट
Plunder

Vanchala's soft features had hardened with pure rage. Her eyes, normally brimming with affection, flickered with spite. Clenched and imprisoned within the vice-like grip of her hands was a letter. A letter that her father had recently inflicted upon her.

He repulsed her. His brutal wickedness had made an indelible mark on her mind. These thoughts swirled in her head the moment she got her hands on his letter. *Why doesn't a snake just bite him and end his miserable existence?* she wondered.

Gangu Naikin shuddered when she saw her niece's expression. A potent combination of fear and sorrow stifled her mind, which was screaming, *Did my Nazuka die during childbirth? Did someone thrash Torappa brutally?*

Meanwhile, Putali, who had just returned to the room after a bath, also sensed this dread when she saw their grave expressions. She was so fearful of Gangu that she couldn't even clothe herself with the blouse, which lay draped on her shoulder. Knowing that Gangu became tyrannical whenever she was afflicted by grief, Putali approached the shrine and fervently prayed, hoping she'd be placated somehow. Gangu blankly stared at the numerous scars on her back.

Outside lounged Soni with her shapely, fair thighs in a cross-legged pose as she let the sun frolic on her lustrous back. Gangu's misery elated her. She gleefully told Vanchala to go ahead and read the contents of the ominous letter.

'Vanchala, read it out once, won't you?' she said. She imagined that the letter contained details about someone having brutally murdered Torappa, which meant Gangu would have to frantically return to her village Gangu hadn't let her sit idle for a single second since she had bought her. The relentless line of customers exhausted her, and she ached for a moment's reprieve.

Vanchala hardened her heart and started to read.

'To, my respected elder sister (who is like my mother), Gangubai, your younger brother Torappa humbly bows before you and salutes you. I wish to inform you that your sister-in-law, Nazuka, with the grace of God…' To regain her fleeting patience, she stopped for a moment – admittedly, with great effort. Her pause sent Gangu's doubt-ridden anxiety skyrocketing while Soni lamented that now, because Torappa hadn't met with an untimely death, she would never get her well-deserved rest.

'…with the grace of God, has borne a son!'

'WHAT?!' Gangu yelled in a moment of supreme joy. On seeing that her sorrows had been dispelled, Putali sighed with no small measure of relief.

'Nazuka begs you to bring a *vajartika,* a pair of floral gold earrings and a fine brocaded *patal*. Also, she insists that this boy and his arrival be celebrated with great pomp and ceremony. So, please send hundred to hundred and fifty rupees immediately. As for myself…' As she read the letter, filled to the brim with selfish and wanton demands, Vanchala seethed with rage and fell silent, as if hit by a bad case of lockjaw. No matter how hard she tried, she could not read any further, Her heart ached.

Gangu, blinded by the joyous news, deviously ignored Vanchala and said, 'I'll send the money by tomorrow. What is the price of money? And, Nazuka, why are you begging, prostrating yourself before someone like me? In fact, I should be grabbing your feet! You have flooded our houschold with joy and light…' Gangu was choking with emotion. Her sepia-tinted eyes cascaded tears of joy. Her body quivered with this sudden burst of inner, barely contained emotion. *When do I send the money? How do I ensure that Nazuka is adorned like a goddess?* Her mind raced.

Soni was agitated after witnessing Gangu's joyous outburst. She feared that in her ecstatic state, Gangu might just decide to exploit her mercilessly. Putali was relaxed. Vanchala, on the other hand, had become cold and uncaring. She wanted to kill. If not her father, Gangu would do. Her mind coursed with these violent thoughts, and she couldn't contain herself. 'Is he a father or a bloody monster?! With an insatiable appetite, a greedy heart – he's a tormentor, a bloody pimp!'

'WHAT?' Gangu suddenly became confrontational.

'I said what I said. A pimp!' Vanchala spat, eager to turn into a sword that would unleash itself on Gangu. And Gangu, cunning as she was, swallowed her anger because the young, beautiful, skilful Vanchala was making her a lot of money. She faked a benign attitude to avoid any further trouble.

'Vanchala, Nazuka may not be your real mother – but she's a mother, regardless. She hasn't wronged you. Your mother had five girls after you. Agreed, a lot of money was borrowed and spent to bring Nazuka into our family – but she was worth every penny. She brought fortune with her. She furthered your father's lineage. She brought Diwali into our house.'

'Yeah, and turned me into *Holi*!' Vanchala erupted. Gangu was furious, since she had to feign helplessness in front of Putali and Soni.

'Not your father – your bloody sins are responsible!' Gangu, who was not used to being patient, regretted the words as soon as they left her mouth. She remembered Vanchala's terrible temper and tried to rein herself in. Her dream of wreathing her brother and sister-in-law with gold was beginning to seem impossible.

'Me… me… me… You accuse *me* of sinning? Tell me the truth, you old hag, was it me?! Wasn't I staying with my husband? Even if he beat me, abused me and threw me out of the house – TWICE – wasn't I the one who dutifully went back? Wasn't I enduring all his beatings like some hapless cattle?! Wasn't I toiling so that he could live well? LOOK – just look at this—' *Clack-clack* went the buttons on her blouse as she snapped them off to reveal the scars on her breasts, her stomach.

'When I couldn't take it any more, I came to my father. And what father? He was a monster, a *rakas*! Both of us – mother and daughter – tried yelling, drilling some sense into him day in and out. He wouldn't let me get a divorce. He wouldn't get divorced either. Forget that, he didn't even let me immolate myself so that I could just die. This went on for three long years. Then came my mother's cousin brother. Spoke many honeyed words. Demanded that I be his instead. Everyone agreed to that match, and in the same vein… Finished. It was your brother who beat him up and drove him out. He would become my husband, right? If he was so righteous, why did he throw his daughter in a *chakla*? Should have simply slit my windpipe with a nail, aborted me instead! Now, in a single day, I acquire ten – and in a month, countless husbands… and that is "righteous", isn't it? You did this – all so you could turn me into a cash cow…' Reaching the peak of her frustration, she bellowed and started to cry.

Gangu, determined to not let the business take a hit, prepared to ply her with false solidarity.

'Vanchala, *Satavi's* mark★ never disappears, no matter how much we bash it against a rock – all that happens is our forehead turns to dust. Because of this mark, Draupadi had to start a household with not one but five husbands! Just take my case…' Vanchala was crying. Soni, whose own sorrows had been stirred by Vanchala's tears, started to cry, too. And Putali, on seeing their tears, was perplexed. Given that this auspicious moment was tarnished by unwarranted sorrow, Gangu's anger had turned into something more ferocious. But she kept quiet because she needed Vanchala's earnings for the next seven to eight days. Only then could she deck her sister-in-law up like a goddess. Celebrate the boy's birth with pomp. To enable that sweet, utopian moment where money would flow like water, Gangu quietly narrated her own tale.

'My husband sold me off to a madam when I was at absolutely no fault. Why? Well, he thought that the piece of land he'd

---

★ Satavi, or Sita, is worshipped during childbirth. If she is displeased she 'marks' the child with a life of misfortune.

mortgaged to get married to me was worth much more; so, he decided to try and get it back. We came to Mumbai to earn money, but we couldn't manage that. He longed for his village, and without it, he couldn't cope. He, too – much like your husband, Vanchala – would fly into a rage and beat me. Thought that I was responsible for him losing his land! In the end, he told me to stay with his sister, saying that he would return after a short trip to his village. Needless to say, he never returned. It was not that he simply died – he had sold me off to his sister! What was more, she wasn't even his sister. She was a madam. That's how husbands are, snakes, each and every one of them.'

Soni agreed with Gangu's monologue. Her life was the same. Tired of her husband's poverty, she had run off with a man. That so-called salaried man turned out to be a pimp. He had sold her off to Gangu.

Vanchala was still crying. Gangu's rhetoric, laced as it was with justifications of pure selfishness, had rekindled her inner fire, and Soni, wanting to ensure that Gangu didn't carry any venom in her heart, sympathetically asked, 'And then what happened?'

'What else could happen? I turned my bones into rickety-sticks for my younger brother. I hollowed myself out so that he wouldn't want for anything. Today, I have a debt of a thousand rupees in my name… but I won't let anything harm him. He—'

'I will not give him a single dime. I won't even let him stand where I spit. That bastard, he'll do the same thing to my younger sister. But I'll get him arrested, and then, after he dies, I will dance *thayya-thayya* on his goddamn grave!' Vanchala shot up suddenly and slammed her feet as she danced with great fury. She hissed, spat and let loose a torrent of abuse before darting out of the room like an arrow.

'Vancha…' Gangu – the Gangu who loved her brother beyond belief, the one who loathed and criticized womankind's existence on principle because of her own past – was frightened at Vanchala's pure, emotional outburst. She turned a pallid, yellowing shade akin to turmeric. She didn't move for a while and simply stared at the open door. And then, as if seared by the hottest fire, she screamed, '*Soneyy*!'

Now determined to destroy Vanchala and recover her losses, she decided to immediately open for business.

'*Soneyy*, get ready. And quickly!'

'But I haven't even bathed, haven't eaten; let's do this in the evening…'

'No, NOW! *Putaley*…' Vanchala's assault had turned her into a *hadal*. Putali was stupefied with fear. She could see the signs of Gangu's transformation. But despite her habit – which was to obey Gangu's orders – she could not lift a single toe. Because for the past seven–eight years, Gangu had never let her go first. When she started, business was always sluggish, resulting in *laas* – that was the belief. If the business went into *laas* today, Gangu wouldn't even spare her a glass of water before she kicked her out, and it was this burning realization that made her resolutely stay right where she was.

On seeing Putali's suddenly defiant attitude, Gangu showered her with abuse. The frightened Putali began relying on Yelamba's grace, praying fervently that Gangu's anger vanished, that she was assuaged somehow. To entice customers, she began blowing streams of red *gulaal* on the bed and then all over the room, gripped by dread because she hadn't had time to complete her puja even as she inched towards the open door.

And Gangu had become incapable of handling the slightest delay. Vanchala's assault had opened a wound and turned her into a terrible tyrant. She wanted a *veshya* who would utter all kinds of obscenities, behave in all sorts of appalling ways to destroy Vanchala. The sight of Putali's muttering and her timidly miserable gait made her explode, '*Arrey*, *oh*, you bloody zebra from Ranibaug… cover up that streaked, pockmarked back of yours… or have you too decided to kill me off… put on that bra, turn around…'

Putali could not undo the damage of her actions so far. Gangu's onslaught ensured that any coherent thoughts in her mind (frayed as it was by many agonies) had flown far, far away. Harrowed, she fervently clutched at her clothes so that she could dress herself. As she desperately tugged at her clothes right at the entrance, she felt a man's gaze settle on her. Her movements were frantic as she struggled to hide the streaks on her body. But it was futile.

On seeing her pathetic state, Soni was filled with pity. But anger surged through every pore of Gangu's body, from her toes to her forehead, and she yelled, 'Let it be. Let it be! Show him – just show him. Move the hem of your sari aside… ugh, you bloody hag.'

Putali didn't obey Gangu because she feared for her future. Instead, she tried being suggestive and used her neck to try and make a gesture. On seeing her invitation, the freeloader instantly left. Gangu started to slice her open with her sharp, abusive tongue, and Putali endured it even as she wiped her tears. Because she had to survive… and survive the longest. She had to eat, drink, beautify herself, get dressed. Then, after that, live the life of a leper and die the death of one – on the road, alone, abandoned.

Time passed by slowly, despondently. People would've received their salaries today, but even then, business was slow. Men sporadically stopped by from here and there, but then moved on. Putali was getting increasingly agitated. *Why didn't Yelamba send all these men to me?* she asked herself even as Gangu's hopes started to wane. But sending a money order to her brother, decking up her sister-in-law with jewels, celebrating the boy's name with great pomp – all of these desires had intensified in her mind. She was hurt because she had to face facts: Vanchala's absence did not bode well for the business. Defeat stared her in the face. And the beautiful, strong Soni was not making any impact either.

'*Soneyy*, will Vanchala come?' On hearing Gangu's sadly uttered question, Soni's happiness and Putali's despair – both had no bounds. They were silent as they pondered upon Gangu's state of mind. Gangu, too, was lost in thought. *Soni will take fifteen to twenty men. At the rate of four to five rupees, she should make about sixty to eighty rupees. Half of that amount will be mine. Putali will add fifteen to twenty rupees to that. The rest? Vanchala will manage.*

'Soni, will Vanchala come?' Gangu asked.

'No, she won't!' Soni answered, triumphant.

'She won't?' Gangu's mind churned violently. She began thinking of ways to put Vanchala to work, when suddenly, as if struck by lightning, she screamed, '*Soney,* get Sidrappa here!'

'I will not.'

'Why not?!' Gangu shouted.

'She will break forever. Might poison herself and die.'

Gangu agreed with Soni. If she did bring him, Vanchala could break forever. The steady flow of money would stop. But then, how could she get her out? What was she to do? Gangu's inner fire burned, hotter than before. She chastised herself. And here, Putali's mind went utterly haywire. If she did not earn anything before the day ended, Gangu would throw her into a whorehouse that was even worse. There, disease or starvation would trample all over her… eventually, leprosy would take her… The premonition of this horrible future made her think that Sidrappa dada should, after all, drag Vanchala by her hair and beat her into submission so that she would finally get to work. She sought an opportunity to summon him and prayed to Yelamba that Gangu's attention be diverted for her to exit.

At that moment, Gangu was convinced that even the beautiful Soni could not attract men to her establishment. Mentally preparing herself to grovel at Vanchala's feet, she walked out. Thinking that this was a sign from the goddess herself, Putali tried making a hasty exit. But before she knew it, three men flooded the doorway. The knowledge that she was better than Putali delighted Soni. Suddenly, Gangu returned. She was pleased because Vanchala had finally appeared from where the girls stayed and was making her way towards them.

Soni took one of the men inside. Gangu's half-share meant that she had freshly minted at least two rupees. She was going to obtain another four rupees from the rest of them. But the urge to quickly make as much money as possible ate at her. For this, she decided to set Soni aside and advertise Vanchala's many qualities to those men instead.

But the men were not paying Gangu any attention. They still stared at the closed door where Soni was. Gangu tried diverting their attention by describing Vanchala's body, bereft of any clothing. She narrated all kinds of scenarios that would be found in the *Kamasutra* in the most vulgar language possible. This was when Vanchala entered, holding the door for support. She was tired. Crying had sapped her.

'Look at this. What a succulent cucumber she is!' The man Gangu had enticed took Vanchala's soft, delicate hand in his, and tried slipping her a five-rupee note. She retreated. Her refusal increased his desire tenfold. When he slipped his hand around her waist instead, Vanchala punched him in his chest with great force. He seemed to enjoy the punch, but Gangu felt its intended impact. The happiness she had experienced earlier turned into vengefulness. Vanchala's words had afflicted her. Gangu was fully stoked by the fires of a cold, unfeeling enmity towards her. Vanchala was worse than a poisonous serpent. Emboldened by these thoughts, she surged forward and gave her a thunderous slap right across her face. 'Wanted to kill my brother, did you… Dance on his grave, will you?'

Vanchala was ready to crush her, too. In fact, she wanted to ask Gangu for some money. She wanted to go watch a movie, but Gangu's vile behaviour enraged her, and she ended up punching this stranger instead.

Both of them stood face to face, their hands entangled in each other's hair in a vice-like grip born out of pure hatred. The men, meanwhile, observed this scuffle with amusement. Gangu, who had decided to fight Vanchala out of a fierce love for her brother, was now calling out to Sidrappa so that he could break all her bones, and Vanchala was giving the crazed, animalistic Gangu a ruthless beating. The two onlookers, upon seeing Vanchala's agility, and subsequently, her inflamed body, were completely smitten.

A few women from the nearby shops streamed out, running towards Gangu's establishment. On seeing this chaotic swarm, Putali and Sidrappa made a beeline towards where the scuffle was.

'*Hato!*' Sidrappa sliced through the crowd. He grabbed Vanchala by her neck and waist and threw her on the bed. The man who was with Soni used this chaos to take advantage of her.

'Who is going in?' Sidrappa's voice was so ominous that the women immediately made themselves scarce. Vanchala lay there, lifeless. She resembled a husk. Her face was pallid, and she stared at the man near the foot of the bed with the white, soulless eyes of a corpse. Soni tried to see if Vanchala was alright, but Sidrappa was a threat that loomed large, keeping her right where she was.

'Ganga, fork over five.' Sidrappa named his price.

'Five?' Gangu was dumbfounded.

'Ten!'

Gangu silently gave him five rupees. He took the money and left, dispersing the crowd on his way out. At the same time, a policeman appeared and did not leave before taking a bribe. Enraged by the ruckus that Gangu had created, the landlord had entered, too. He brandished his cudgel. 'What is this *tamasha?* You don't pay on time, you don't kick this Putali out. If you don't want to do business, then get out of here at once! Get out!' He'd mentioned Putali's name to extract more money. Gangu understood his motives and gestured at him, hoping that he wouldn't say another word. Instead, he screamed.

'Give me today's rent – for the room, for electricity and the furniture. Right now!'

Gangu handed him three rupees. When everything had quietened down, Soni emerged and silently ferried the other customer in. She couldn't tell anyone that Vanchala was comatose or that Putali was fervently trying to attract the hordes of men that passed by to assuage Gangu. Because she knew that after today, Gangu would throw her into a brothel that was way worse. Grotesque visions of that abysmal environment flickered before her eyes. Gangu's share, the money required for the upkeep of the place, rent for the room and bed, in addition to whatever the police and the goons would take anyway – and her price? Only one rupee, or twelve annas!

सक्तमजुरी
Hard Labour

The sun was boiling hot. On the molten tar road, the crowd from the second shift was briskly running past, their legs not breaking stride. As soon as they came within earshot, Fernandes (who ran a gambling grift) enthusiastically yelled, 'Put ten down, win twenty instead… put five down, win ten!' It was all an act, of course. He was exhausted by all the hawking he'd had to do since morning.

With that, his companions swung into action, too. Sikandar Sindhi played the role of a Gujarati man. Kassim Ali perfectly imitated the cadence of a *bhaiyya* and Sambha would adopt a Konkani or Satari dialect when speaking Marathi. Despite that, not a single workman stopped. Not a single rupee had been wagered. Their temporary enthusiasm ran dry pretty quickly, and everyone on the lookout believed that the curse of Fernandes's wife had doomed them. They claimed that Fernandes had violently beaten her within an inch of her life for absolutely no reason.

Amidst these people was Fernandes's thirteen-year-old son, Daniel. He was dejected and agitated at the same time, and he looked at every passerby with hope in his eyes. *Now we'll be in business. Then, my old man will take me to a restaurant, then he'll finally get me something to eat.* But every incoming man heartlessly brushed past the boy and his empty stomach. Every time his father was ignored, Daniel would waver and come dangerously close to tears.

Last night, his mother and father had had one of their most harrowing fights. Fernandes had savagely beaten his mother into a comatose state. The children went hungry. To avoid her curses from infecting his business, Fernandes hadn't spent a single penny on food yet. Daniel couldn't even stand properly because of this. Having to stand in the rising heat without a single morsel of food inside him made his head spin. His stomach quivered with hunger. His eyes were droopy, about to shut. He felt like sitting down and abandoning it all. But if he told his father he was hungry or had left his place to satiate his hunger with some water from the restaurant across the road, then… then the frustrated, irate Fernandes would soundly thrash him. This was why he didn't sit. Didn't let the juju get to the business. Didn't look at the sky to gleefully observe the kite fights. Didn't steal the glass-dusted strings or retrieve the fallen ones. He just looked at everybody who passed them by. His eyes didn't stray from the prize. His father had sentenced him to a lifetime of hard labour, and he endured it like a convict.

His father played with the cards in his hand, muttering, 'Come one, come all. Don't just observe, don't think too much! Put ten down, win twenty instead… put five down, win ten instead…'

But those who were in a rush didn't even glance in his direction. They didn't pay attention to old man Khaitan's advances. Daniel's resolve was fruitless, and every time someone passed by, Fernandes's spirits would sink. The whole of last week had been plagued with bad luck, and its memory flashed before his eyes.

Since salary day was still a long way away, he was desperate for money. His little gambling operation couldn't sustain him. At home, a war brewed between husband and wife, with conflict always a second away. Worse still was the fact that a shrewd gambler had won their entire pot the last time. Fernandes fought him in a bid to get the money back. His seven companions assisted him, too, but somehow, he overwhelmed them all and reached the police station. There, he convinced the police to pursue them relentlessly. This was why they couldn't afford to stick to a street corner for too long and had no regular customer pool.

This adverse situation, coupled with his lack of success, had made him extremely irritable. He brooded and seethed with rage. The moment he reached home empty-handed, his wife would clash with him, and as usual, he would remain criminally silent. Because he could see the situation inside his house. Three of his six children were ill. One had a perpetual case of dysentery. Two of them were infected with rabies. They would squirm, pant, be out of breath and retch repeatedly. His wife couldn't devote too much attention to them because she was pregnant – for the seventh time.

He couldn't get them any medicine either. His business was slow. But he refused to sit at home and mope. He thought that one of these days, he'd hit gold. Last night, feeling hopeful, he'd told his wife, 'Take them to the dispensary tomorrow…'

His tone was meek. He had condemned himself, and at the same time, felt sorry for her.

But she aggressively let fly with a searing torrent of verbal abuse. For the whole of last week, since there was no money coming in, he hadn't paid any attention to the affairs inside the house while his children's health had deteriorated, so her anger was warranted. So, he kept his cool. He quietly explained, 'Look, we owe the grocer forty rupees, with a ten-rupee interest. If I don't pay, then the loan goes up to fifty rupees. And then, the interest rate will increase to twelve and a half rupees. The business isn't working. The police hound me. What should I do? Tell me!'

She abused him without considering his state, without thinking about what he would go through every day. To her, he was a demon who could only think of putting one child after another inside her. Why didn't he give her any new clothes or a morsel of good food? In the most vulgar way possible, she told him that he was nothing but a lustful animal who'd preyed on her. Then, she cried before insulting him further.

His state of mind, damaged as it was because of their general plight, could not withstand that attack, and he beat her. She, too, began tacking on the abuse with each successive blow and invoked his numerous flaws. Eventually, she slumped to the floor, unconscious. The sound of his children crying, the blind haze that clouded his mind as he beat her senseless, her acidic tongue – all of it took a toll and left him chronically plagued with anxiety. To calm his mind, he went to a hut nearby and took another loan to buy some booze. After that, he spent the rest of the night in a drunken stupor. In his quest to terrorize the slum, he was beaten, shoved and repeatedly thrown to the filthy, muddy ground. He lay there all night long.

When he returned home in the morning, his wife had a fever. His children, ill as they were, had vomited and stained the sheets with excrement. This horrendous sight shattered his heart. He woke Daniel up and joined his companions. At the rate of four annas to a rupee, he scrounged up ten rupees for the pot and plied his trade. But now, it was almost evening. Not many had come in. He rapidly changed their spot to make a quick buck but to no avail. His troupe was distressed. They blamed him for beating his wife.

Plagued by anger and frustration, sorrow and hunger, they sat near a railway crossing. There were a couple of mills and some factories nearby. And while this place definitely boded well for their business, the threat of being caught and arrested was greater, too. This was a risky location. The afternoon sky assailed them with heat from above. Below, the streets smouldered. Gusts of abysmally hot wind entered their mouths, their throats and sucked every drop of moisture from their bodies. They were thirsty. Stomachs churned. The winds whipped them, each lash like a lightning strike. Rivulets of sweat gushed from their bodies. Their necks strained from keeping their heads aloft as they scanned the crowds for the police. Their eyes were engulfed in flames. They'd kept their mouths running without any food or water for a while now. Their heads were pounding. Their mouths, their hair were caked with dirt. Even their sweat had dried up because of the heat. Hot vapours issued from their mouths and noses. And even though his throat ached, Fernandes kept talking like it was his last breath,

'Put ten down, win twenty instead... put five down, win ten instead... Test your luck. Don't keep watching... Don't think too much!'

And as soon as he stopped, Sikandar Sindhi would ask him in Gujarati, '*Arrey*, brother, if I put some money down, will I get any back?' Fernandes would then answer in his best impression of an indignant, righteous man – the same one he'd used countless times since the morning – and tell him, 'I've been doing this for fifteen years. Don't believe me? Ask this man here...'

With that, old man Khaitan, who played the interested gambler's role, had grabbed the arms of an unsuspecting worker and dragged him towards Fernandes. But it was all in vain. The man slapped aside Khaitan's black, sweaty hands and escaped swiftly. The four of them were crestfallen as they watched his retreating back and hurled abuses in his direction. Fernandes, on the other hand, was looking at yet another workman, saying, 'Let him go, ask this *bhaiyya*...' and Sikandar Sindhi, in Gujarati, asked their *bhaiyya* impersonator, Kassim Ali a few questions. Then, he held out a rupee from his mighty two-rupee hoard.

'Don't think about it too much – go for it!' Fernandes urged Sikandar on. The *bhaiyya* told him to set the money down. Old man Khaitan backed them up with enthusiasm, and Sindhi took a good look around, stepped forward and put his bet down on a card, saying, 'This one!'

'This one?'

'Yes, that's the one!'

An utterly bored Fernandes lifted the same card for the umpteenth time and showed it to the exhausted Sikandar Sindhi, who didn't want to speak another word. He impatiently licked his cracked, parched lips and said, '*Bassha*.'

'King. It is a king, correct?'

'That's right!'

Fernandes dextrously played with the card and looked at the passers-by with pitiful hope in his eyes. But the supposed targets of their little scheme would merely laugh and leave. Despite that, Sindhi kept the charade going.

'I've decided!'

'You have? Oh! You won!'

'I won!' He let his voice reach the workmen nearby, who he hoped would be enticed into playing a round. Old man Khaitan tried luring a workman who had approached them, saying, 'That bloody Gujarati, just see, he's quite lucky. Won ten rupees at the price of just one! Look, look!'

But no one looked. The man, in fact, had shaken Khaitan off and was moving away from them when Fernandes told Kassim, 'Ay, *bhaiyya,* you're really smart. You won some money. Why don't you convince your fellow man here to try his luck?' However, before Kassim could get any closer, the *bhaiyya* had bolted. Kassim loudly yelled in his wake, 'Oy motherfucker, come back!'

All these antics were being performed to attract customers. But success eluded them. Their hearts sank. Their limbs drooped with sheer exhaustion. The heat seared their bodies. With no food in their stomachs, they couldn't even bear to stand. *We should eat something, get our spirits back up and then get back to the grind,* they all thought. But Fernandes didn't budge. He mumbled as if possessed. The cards flew around in his hand, and he kept trying to get someone to play…

Time sapped them and made them despondent. Daniel, with his unseasoned, undeveloped mind and body, cried. He longed for his comatose mother. A morbid thought occurred to him – *Had she passed away?* This made him cry even more. His hunger surged anew. The tears amplified. He frantically attempted to wipe them away, fearing that his father would see him. He tried keeping his eyes on the road instead, which had become a blur amidst the curtain of ever-cascading tears. Like Daniel, the others were distressed, too. Fernandes started to understand his wife's plight. Without giving her any new clothes to wear, or good food to eat, he had beaten her. He had treated her like a tool that alleviated some of the strife: both within and without his mind. He had harassed her as she starved. Now, he had to make her happy. He had to give her new clothes. He had to give her a lot of money. Inspired by this fleeting sense of purpose, he screamed again, 'Put ten down, win twenty instead… put five down, win ten instead…'

However, not one of his companions joined him. Each of them wallowed in their own grief. Old man Khaitan had been thrown out of the house by his sons because he had a drinking problem and beat his daughters-in-law… Sikandar Sindhi remembered the massacre in Karachi, haunted by how his younger brother had betrayed him. One after the other, the sirens inside the mills went off. Waves of workers spilt out on the streets. This gave them a newfound sense of hope. They mumbled to each other in excitement. Kassim Ali snagged a *bhaiyya* passing by and asked him for tobacco before attempting to entice him into playing a round. But nobody listened. The workers rushed past them. They were crushed under despair's hideous foot, agitated beyond belief, and Sikandar Sindhi, in his anguish, suddenly spluttered, 'Brother, shut it down. Today, we don't have any luck on our side. Come, let's get something to eat… something to drink…'

On hearing Sikandar Sindhi's words, Fernandes thought about whether his wife was alive, or worse, dead. He furiously retorted, 'Shut your mouth, or I will break it.'

'What did you say?'

'Bastard, my wife and children are dying, and all you can think of is food? I already have the grocer's fifty-rupee loan on my head. And you? We do all the hard work, and all you want is to stuff your face, eh?'

'My wife was snatched by brigands. Exploited. Murdered. I saw my children killed before my very eyes. So what if God also takes yours away from you?'

'What did you say?' Fernandes was stung by the cold apathy that seemed to come so easily to him. He surged to his feet and shoved him, asking, '*Shaitan,* do you have a heart or any pity whatsoever?'

Sikandar, who had been starving since morning – and who loathed the idea of a hard, penniless life – had invoked Fernandes's wrath. He took out his frustration on him. Khaitan, Kassim Ali and Sambha broke them up. Only Daniel, who was terrified of his father's anger, remained right where he was. He watched the brawl with rapt attention. The fracas was their way of displacing the discontent they had been feeling so far, but fate threw a spanner in the wheels. An ominous whistle blew, and even as it blew, they broke it up and frantically scanned the area for danger. The police jeep had parked very close to them. Two policemen had already raised their sticks threateningly at their group.

'Come here!' The sahib motioned for Fernandes to come closer, and Fernandes mentally prepared himself. He planned to tell the sahib of his woes, prostrate himself at his feet and beg for forgiveness so that he could save them all. The sahib slapped Fernandes's haggard face and dismissively motioned for him to stand aside. That resounding slap made Fernandes snap out of his haze. The sahib hurled an abuse and called Sikandar forward.

Sindhi marched towards the sahib with his head held high. In a resounding voice, he said, 'Don't abuse me. Throw me in jail if you have to!'

The sahib's mood immediately turned foul. He slapped him twice. Two thunderous slaps, one after the other. Sindhi clenched his fists and raged. 'Why are you beating me? Take me to jail… Does your father dictate the law, eh? Who the fuck do you think you are?' These retorts made the sahib fly into a rage. He unleashed a barrage of kicks and baton strikes on the hapless Sindhi and didn't stop until he'd collapsed to the ground. The sahib, determined to set an example, thrashed the rest of them, too.

'Shall we take them in?' asked a havildar, tucking in his shirt that had come out amidst all the beating and exertion.

'Take them!' the sahib said, and the havildar obliged, kneeing them and edging them towards the jeep.

'Good riddance… This fucking life is just hard, unending labour anyway.' Sambha moved forward to get into the vehicle.

'Wait…' The sahib assailed Sambha with a particularly vile insult and made him lower the foot that he had raised to climb in.

'5520, frisk him.' 5520 complied and handed over the ten rupees that he found on him.

'Beat these sons of bitches some more and chase them off…'

The havildar beat each of them on their posteriors and drove them away like sheep.

The seven of them and Daniel made their way towards the slum. No one spoke. Fernandes loathed the idea of going home because he didn't have the heart to face his wife empty-handed. If she had risen, then she might provoke him to the point where she wouldn't rise again.

Daniel lagged behind and dragged his feet as he walked. He thought that his father would beat him for not whistling in time to warn them. Because when the jeep passed by him, his eyes had been looking to the sky, enraptured by the kite strings cutting each other.

भूक

Hunger

The rain was aggressive, blocking all sight as it cascaded down. It had reduced the best of them to a sorry state. Those who were living from hand to mouth were plagued by starvation. The rain's assault had softened them like wet earth, and disease spread far and wide like freshly grown grass. Every house had someone who was ill.

The fisherwoman Bhagu had been laid low by cold and fever. Both her sons were hungry and vexed because of her illness, which accompanied the persistent rain. After eating whatever they got by begging for it, they sat at the foot of her bed listlessly. They got through the day with hunger and sorrow as their constant companions.

Sometimes, when her fever broke and she managed to come to her senses, the sight of her starving, miserable, tearful children would break her, little by little. She'd wipe her tear-laden eyes. And she would become distressed despite her faith, imploring God to stop this rain and make her fever disappear.

Finally, the lord of rain heard her prayers. The sun's companion left, taking with him the rain that enriched the

Earth. Just like that, the fever and exhaustion in her body receded. She woke with a start and called out to her stupefied children, 'Bhika, Satva – come here, my babies…'

On hearing their mother, the lethargy and sorrow that had seeped into their bodies vanished. They spryly came to her side and embraced her. She looked at her elder son and said, 'Bhika, go to the village. Tell the *patlin** that your mother has asked for two measures of flour.'

'Mother, please, no – I don't feel like going to her. As soon as she sees me at her door, she shoos me off like a rabid dog…'

'Bu' she s'ill gives it,' the smooth, round-cheeked, button-nosed and bush-plum black-haired Satva said. The nectar on his tongue hadn't melted yet. Her mind rejoiced at the sound of his sweet words, accentuated by his lisp.

She consoled Bhika, 'Now if you show up at her house every day, what do you think she'll do? Treat you like her son-in-law and serve you while telling you to help yourself? Feed you *puran-polis*? Everyone is sapped during these trying times. Don't grumble. Go to her…'

'No, tell me if I can get it from somewhere else.'

'She's the only one who'll give you anything – she's the village head! If she doesn't feel sorry for you, who will?'

'Anyone else will do.'

'Just go to her. Otherwise, she'll say that I've become too arrogant. Take that vessel. And that cloth.' Her enthusiasm receded. She realized how tired she was. She fell silent. Bhika took the items and stepped outside. His skin shimmered black like oil. He was snub-nosed and had sunken eyes but also

* Female village chief

possessed a tall, hulking frame. He ran off in the direction of the village as he played with the abundant hair on his head.

Satva, meanwhile, placed his soft hand on her neck and said, 'Mum, shu' I go to Thaku aunty? She gives me blead erryday…'

'We shouldn't eat at her house. Our caste will be violated…' Upon remembering Thaku's kindness, she did not poison his mind with casteist thoughts. Embarrassed, she stopped talking.

'So then, shu' I go?'

'Go.' Upon hearing his mother's instruction, he ran off in his oversized pyjamas. All she could see was his little head bobbing in the distance. She pressed her own aching head with both her hands as she watched him go. Tears of pride flowed from her eyes. Her face, otherwise dried out by the fever, swelled with joy.

After some time, her Ram–Laxman duo returned. Bhika's face was downcast. He stood there with a vessel full of curry in one hand and a bundle of flat, unleavened bread in the other. Assuming that the *patlin* had given him an earful, she took the vessel and the bundle from his hands, saying, 'Sit, my prince, sit here.'

She took his hand, made him sit on the floor and lovingly stroked his back. 'Now, let me serve my boy…'

He was disheartened after enduring the *patlin*'s humiliation, but Satva exploded with delight. He'd hoarded some piping hot ragi flatbread and a chutney made of dried prawns in his bulging, gigantic pyjamas. He held it close to his stomach protectively, thinking that Bhika would ask him for it.

She dragged herself to the stove and brought back the zinc plate resting on it along with a pail of water. Pouring the curry on the plate, she said, 'Eat up, my love! Someone born into poverty shouldn't have such intelligence. Eat…' She held Satva close. The touch of his babyish body made her heart overflow with love and tenderness. She repeatedly kissed his dirt-stricken head. Upon seeing his mother praising Satva like this, Bhika was perplexed. His hand, which would expertly knead food into bite-sized morsels, lay still and lifeless. She did not miss that and stroked his back with affection again. She sprinkled him with the tears of life that streamed from her eyes and beckoned him to eat. And just like that, with this new-found encouragement, he consumed his food and somehow savoured it despite it being stale, coarse fare.

Satva was eating with great gusto. He was waiting for the moment when Bhika would step outside. Because after Bhika left, he would give his mother half of the piping hot flatbread. But Bhika's eyes were always on him. After their mother had stroked his back, he had become fearless and was now thinking that Satva might have something delicious in his hands after all. So, he asked, 'What do you have there?'

'Flat blead. Made of ragi for mum. Hot. You eat 'uickly. Mum wants.' He removed the bread that he had kept close to his stomach and set it on their mother's lap.

She laughed when she saw him express such love for her. After kissing his smooth, round cheeks she divided the flatbread into three pieces and handed the boys a piece each while slowly nibbling on the third one.

Bhika took a piece of pickle that he'd hidden in his pocket and gave it to their mother – much like Satva had – in a bid to earn her praise. Knowing how he always clamoured for food, this act brought fresh tears to her eyes. She caressed his head as she tried holding her tears back, but it was futile. So, she faked a cough instead, holding the hem of her sari against her mouth. Bhika nimbly leapt from his position to fetch her some water. In that moment, she managed to wipe her tears away, and with immense love, told him, 'My baby, you just eat first. Then give some to Satva! Become an earning member of the family soon!'

Bhika hated the curry. It was a tepid mixture created by taking some from ten different households. He hated the stale, rock-hard morsels of flatbread, too, but ate them because he was starving. His mother, who loved her children more than she did her own life, who knew of his enormous appetite and saw the dissatisfaction and anguish on his face, resolved to go to the river. She told Bhika, 'Bhika, we are going to the river today. Go check the water level and come back.'

'On my way!' He was so ecstatic that he stopped looking for ways to divide that rock-hard fare. He immediately drank some water and ran outside. Satva, who loved the river, ran after him, his neck wobbling. *Shouldn't have brought this up while they were eating,* she thought, her conscience pricked by guilt. As it was, she was having trouble eating. Being aware of it didn't help; she couldn't swallow another morsel. She kept her share back in the basket, cleaned up the mess, and holding her head in her hands, sat in the doorway.

Before she knew it, her Ram–Laxman appeared. An excited Bhika, amidst all his huffing and puffing, delivered the news, '*Aai*, the water level has fallen, let's go. Catch some fish. Today, we will definitely get some eel.'

'Eel?!' Her astonishment silenced her, and she joined her hands in supplication, looked at the sky and said, 'Oh, Bal

Munja*... may your mouth be sweetened, may we get what we desire.'

'We will definitely get it!' both the boys exclaimed. Her feelings were a blend of excitement and fear – excitement at seeing their confidence, and fear that there wouldn't be any eel waiting for them. So, she told her children, 'Go, go and play. When the water recedes below the stone, then come back and tell me. Go!'

The children ran off, and she began thinking about the eel. How Bhika would be delighted while eating it, how his face would light up at the dinner table, how his blood would pump robustly if he ate it for a couple of days, how his strength – sapped because of starvation – would return. All these thoughts swirled in her head. And her children, energized by these hopeful signs, were running back to her periodically, informing her about each pebble inside the river, practically bringing the vision of the river to life in her mind's eye. She was captivated by their intelligence, their wit. She would sacrifice anything for her sun and moon. And just like that, her parched body filled up with strength and enthusiasm.

It was exactly five when the water finally fell to the level that she wanted. Having distributed their baggage equally amongst the three of them, she arrived at the river with her sons trailing behind her.

The river's turbid water was flowing with tremendous speed. Its banks were littered with slime and filth. Her feet were repeatedly getting wedged in slippery patches or mucky puddles, making her slip, fall and get her hands wet as she struggled.

* A local deity

Despite that, she kept trudging onward while scrutinizing the ground. Her hands cramped because of the excess moisture seeping into them. The bones in her legs ached. Whenever the icy, cool wind fleetingly touched her, the entirety of her would shiver. Her throbbing head now ached with a newfound intensity. Her heavy eyelids obscured her vision. Despite this, she moved forward. Because now, she had vowed to feed her sons and could not give up.

Bhagu was dealing grievous blows to her own body with every step. Her children, giddy with joy, were giggling behind her. Like blooming flowers on an evergreen vine, they exuded happiness, telling each other about what ghosts lived in which pond and where the torch-bearing Vetala danced on moonless and full moon nights, throwing stones at one of the many water snakes lying in the mud and then laughing at the plight of the creature as it struggled, rendered powerless by the river's force.

'*Arrey*, look at that…' A tiny, grass-green snake was making its way before them. Bhika ran with the net on his back and swiftly bent down, caught the snake by its mouth and held it aloft. Looking at the snake's lifeless struggle, Satva laughed and clapped his hands gleefully. He kept asking Bhika whether he could hold the snake, but Bhika, amidst bouts of laughter, refused to hand it over. Satva, agitated that he wasn't getting his way despite pleading, began swiping at Bhika's hand. Bhika would expertly swat his hand away, hold the snake high and yell, 'Don't hold it, it'll bite you. You'll die…'

When the commotion caused by her sons reached Bhagu's numbed mind, she stood and looked behind her. On seeing them playing with the snake, she screamed in fright, 'You fool, Bhikya, throw it away, throw it—' Bhika threw away the snake, and she softly admonished him, 'Don't just pick up everything you see…'

'But, *Aai*, he doesn't bite,' Bhika said, seeing that her anger had dissipated.

And then Satva proclaimed rather boldly, 'Humans don' die cause o' it. And if you just make a paste of some nut grass and drink it…'

She turned around and began walking, knowing that taking this any further would result in a full-blown argument between the brothers as they showed off their knowledge regarding medicinal plants. Satva took this chance to murmur enviously. 'If I sees it then I, too, 'ill not give it to you…'

'But you will never see it.'

'Will too.' Satva was green with envy by now. All his energy was concentrated in his gaze as he scrutinized every pebble and stone, tiny dent and crevice. He saw innumerable forms of life that he had never seen before. But he couldn't find what he was searching for. Besides that, Bhika was provoking him, and he was getting provoked, too. If this had gone on for a while longer, Satva would've begun bawling, but suddenly, he saw a large, multi-hued, glimmering python near the pit where his mother was standing. He screamed, feeling the thrill of victory combined with concern for his mother, '*Aai*, lun, lun, lun away…'

She was still standing obliviously as her children yelled and pulled her away. All of them peered into the pit. In there lay a writhing mass of colourful snakes, coiled, encircled and entwined with each other, as though a dhobi had piled a heap of saris together after beating, thrashing and wringing them dry. A shiver went down her spine upon witnessing this vile, horrific sight. She quaked with fear. But her sons were delighted and looked on, full of excitement. They didn't move despite their mother's attempts to drag them away. She was extremely frightened, and angry at their pluckiness. She didn't utter a word, fearful that the snakes would hear them, and continued pulling her boys away.

A keen desire had formed in the boys' minds – a desire to throw a barrage of stones at the snakes. They bent and looked for ammunition. But she wasn't letting them do any of that. After getting away from the pit, she said, 'One mustn't speak before a snake. One must not hit them with stones; they hold the pain within. Vow to take revenge.'

'If 'e bites, I'll eat some limon leaves…' Satva said. Her heart trembled with fear at those words. She flicked him on the head. Her skeletal fingers stung him, and Bhika, on seeing that his mother had hit Satva, couldn't help but let out a laugh.

'Shut up!' she yelled, fearful that his melodious laughter would reach the snakes. This made them laugh even harder, and with a mixture of dread and rage, she pulled them further away. They laughed, and she continued to tremble. Her fear had taken root during her childhood – when her mother had met her demise because of a snakebite – and continued to this day.

The fear didn't diminish, despite them moving a considerable distance away. To help get rid of this feeling, she readied everything to catch some fish. With Bhika by her side, she entered the knee-deep water and began working. After some time, she was so engrossed that her mind forgot the entire spectacle.

Time passed. The blue sky changed its hue. The sun was setting. She felt feverish, cold. Every bone in her body ached due to her labours. Her veins throbbed. The net attached to her waist filled up. Bhika's basket was laden with sizeable fish. Satva languished on a rock. He was bored of playing about in the muck that the river had brought in. He sat there, his arms and legs caked with mud. Hungry. Bhika was tired, too. He said, '*Aai*, shall I go and sell these?'

'Go, go quickly. After that's done, go to Nana's shop and get some rice. And I'll trap some fish for us. Run.'

Bhika happily began imagining the meal of piping hot rice and fish that awaited him. 'Now if we manage to find that eel, then we're talking—'

'Eel? Sighting one in this river is like catching a glimpse of God; it's so rare…'

'But it appears during the flood, doesn't it? You said it yourself.'

'It does. But you need luck.'

'Then, we'll definitely find it today.' Bhika climbed out of the water. He transferred the fish from the bag hanging at her waist to his shallow basket. He handed the bag back to her, put the basket on his head, stood up and said, 'I'll be off. You'll find the eel.'

'Go. Don't babble so much.' She was frightened of the wave of joy coursing through her. Bhika began walking. And she started to cast her net in the hope that it would snag an eel. And drew it back in.

An alarm went off in Bhika's mind as he neared the pit where they had encountered the snake-heap. He widened his eyes, looking at the path and everything around him. When he didn't see anything, he picked up a stone and stood over the pit. There was a blackish snake still in there, considerably fat but not too long. The other snakes had left. On seeing it, he immediately thought that if this ravenous snake managed to reach the path, it would not rest without biting his mother. With this thought in mind, he put down the basket, took careful aim and pelted the snake with stones. His barrage caused the old snake, who had been rendered lifeless by the flood, to fall back into the swiftly flowing river and disappear.

A frightened Bhika searched for it from afar. He was motivated by a fearful thought: injured snakes vow to take revenge on those who attack them. He blindly threw a fresh load of stones pell-mell into the water, afraid that the snake would appear before his mother and take revenge.

He remembered that he had to sell the fish before his fear threatened to consume him. He would only get a handsome price for his wares if he managed to make it before people prepared for dinner. Otherwise, there would be no customers, and even if there were, he wouldn't break even. With this realization, he forgot everything else and ran like his life depended on it. This also made him stumble at every corner, and some fish fell out of the basket. He didn't even have the presence of mind to pick them up. Out of breath, he finally entered the village.

He hawked his wares in each gully, bellowing as he passed through. Tearing up at the thought of all the fish that had fallen out, he was shrewd when selling the rest of his goods. He lured in customers by invoking his hapless mother and her illness. He hoped that the next snare would net her an eel. She, in turn, was throwing snares out willy-nilly, praying that she'd land a rich, succulent eel so that her boys could feast on something potent. Something full of life. And with every throw of the net, the river surged and bestowed her with a variety of gifts.

Fever reigned supreme in her veins. Sledgehammers pounded her head from within. Her eyes drooped, and her mind had glazed over with the thought of snaring an eel. And then, in this haze, her net suddenly felt a pull. Her eyes, heavy because of the fever, suddenly sparkled. With great hope and tenderness, she drew the net in. Upon seeing the reddish-brown, inky form of the eel in the net, she was satisfied. She knew that the spunky eel would thrash around with great force if she made any sudden tugging movements, so she lifted the net gently and slowly exited the water. She whispered to the lazing Satva, 'Satva, come, take that big basket. Go on, run!'

She hadn't yet set the snare down or changed the soaking wet rags that were attached to her waist. She wasn't looking at the net in her hand or at the stumbling, weeping Satva, who followed her. She was irritated with him, fearing that the eel would slip away. As they moved towards their house, she put some distance between herself and Satva. Otherwise, his voice would provoke the eel.

After stepping in, she delicately tied the net around a peg and changed out of her soaking clothes. She told Satva to stay quiet, and in a feverish haze, found some matches. There was no oil in the bottle or the lamp, so she took the wick out of the lamp, threw it in with a bunch of twigs and lit a fire under the earthen stove. She layered the bottom of the stove with cow-dung cakes, and in that blindingly smoky, hazy house, she cautiously freed the eel and laid it low with a blow to the head. Cut it systematically. Made tiny pieces of its fleshy middle portion, washed them and put them in an earthen pot on the stove. After this entire ordeal, her mind was finally at ease. This was when she remembered Satva.

She pulled him close and began waiting for Bhika. Satva fell asleep on her fevered lap, and as she caressed him, she kept listening keenly for Bhika's approaching footsteps.

As soon as she heard Bhika outside, her gaze swept over to Satva. She shook him gently, saying, 'My child, wake up. Look, your older brother's here. Now I'll make warm rice. My baby will eat his fill of rice. Fish. Wake up.'

Her affection overflowed as she looked at her soft, round-cheeked son. She didn't want him to sleep on an empty stomach. But Satva didn't open his eyes. He had cried too much, was too exhausted, and it felt snug beside the fire. He was in a deep sleep.

Bhika gave her the money he'd earned. He put down the remnants of their fishy haul in front of her and quickly ran outside. He'd sneakily taken a rupee from their earnings to purchase some roasted chickpeas for himself and wanted to savour them.

She prepared two plates as soon as the nutritious eel curry was done cooking. She upturned a large portion into Bhika's plate from the pot and set aside a generous serving for Satva. Then, she kept trying to wake Satva while calling out to Bhika.

On hearing her call, the hungry Bhika appeared instantly. He sat down to eat. The stove's fire illuminated him as he wolfed down the morsels of fish, demolishing the massive heap on his plate. His impressive appetite pleased her as she fed bite-sized morsels to Satva, who was now half-awake. He opened his mouth for a few bites before shutting it for good. This made her angry. The fever had killed her appetite, but she began putting tiny portions in her mouth to give Bhika company.

After the meal was over, she covered the leftovers properly to keep the cat from stealing them and went to bed with her sons by her side. Both were fast asleep. The fever made her tremble. Her throat was dry. A wave of nausea welled up from her stomach. She felt like vomiting.

Outside, the rain cascaded heavily. The wind lashed at her house. Bhika was rudely awakened by a steady stream of rainwater that had breached their decrepit roof. Wanting to share the dream he'd had, he called out to his mother. '*Aai*…'

'What is it, my child?' she groaned.

'Did that black snake cross your path again?'

'Why, did you see it in your dream?' she asked, wanting to soothe him.

'Yes. But I pelted it with stones and drove it off. How did it manage to come close to you, then? How did it bite you; didn't it flow away…?'

'But it didn't bite me.'

'Why were you screaming? Didn't you see it in the water, coming towards you? It was dead, more or less.'

'No!' Pure fear exploded inside her. It filled every pore. She began quaking. Her body was drenched with sweat. The little strength she had inside her receded. Stumbling, she clumsily made her way to the covered pot, grabbed it and peered inside as her hands touched the mass within.

Every steamed piece now looked like snake meat to her. Felt like it, too. Somewhere inside, her hand brushed against the head, which was definitely a snake's. A deep terror infected her as she vividly imagined what her sons might do if they found out what they'd consumed. Her heart sank.

'Satva... Bhi... Bhikaaaaaaaaa!' she wailed and collapsed. And as her body hit the floor, the flame of life – sustained by the love she had for her sons – was extinguished forever.

Bhika, sated by the meal, called out to her. Satva awoke with a start as he heard his brother's howls. He was burning up since he'd been clinging to his mother's feverish body.

The frenzied wind whipped through the trees and lashed against their ramshackle house. A black sea formed in the skies above, threatening to spill over at any moment. The moon had sunk inside this heavenly abyss and was nowhere in sight. Its light waned; it became non-existent. Everything turned to black.

आई

Mother

The teacher who had arrived to take the class was so compelling in his teaching of the poem titled 'Mother', that the mood of every unfortunate child was uplifted. After completing the session, the teacher left, and one by one, the children escaped from the poem's clutches, falling back down to earth. That strange, marvellous feeling receded like the tide. The children returned to their original state. But the poem refused to leave Pandu's mind. He'd started to see his mother as the 'beacon of love' that the poem declared her to be. He saw the greatness in her. It was as if his boyish innocence had escaped from its prison. A great weight lifted off his shoulders. He felt like laughing, playing, making mischief like he'd never felt before. All his classmates suddenly felt like his best friends. He laughed, taking in the chaos that was his classroom.

The thuggish kids quickly took notice when they saw the normally sullen, reclusive Pandu enjoy himself. Lakhu, notorious for pulling pranks and causing mayhem, began behaving like a skittish lamb. Pandu watched these antics and forgot any animosity he might have harboured. Instead, he clutched at his sides and laughed uncontrollably.

'Lakhu, look at that—'

Namu, whose hairstyle mimicked Dilip Kumar's, was laughing hysterically. Snot dripped from his nose onto his lips. Of course, he was unaware.

'Snot-kumar…'

Before Lakhu could continue, Namu quickly wiped off the snot, and the classroom echoed with laughter. The deceitful, sly Bhaga had taken notice of this blooming friendship between Pandu and Lakhu. He screamed, 'Lakhya, you fucker, I'll tell your father – you made up with this Pandya, spoke to him, even put your hand around his neck! He told us not to talk to this whoreson. He's a nasty bastard. Come on, swear that you won't talk to him!'

'I swear!'

Lakhu removed his hand from Pandu's shoulder with a sudden jolt and shoved him away. The children clapped and raised hell. The well-loved Kala, who had the ability to return the choicest abuses to his own parents – with interest – quickly said, 'So, boys, my mum says that Pandya's mum's a hooker! She's with some foreman now, he's like this…'

Kala stood on his toes and puffed his lips and frame to illustrate the size of this massive foreman. The boys laughed again. Pandu returned to his seat and mutely endured the abuse directed at him. These 'beloved' children, who belonged to mean-spirited families, pecked at him like crows. Told him about how his mother was slandered in their homes. He responded in kind. This new avatar of his angered them. A couple of them shoved him around. Bhaga incited a few of the boys under his command and set them on him. A full-scale brawl erupted, but before it could continue, the school bell rang, marking the end of the day. Everyone grabbed their slate boards and bags before running towards the exit. Bhaga, in his typical thuggish form, straightened his collar, puffed up his chest and told Pandu, 'You bastard pimp, come out! I'll murder you!'

Bhaga brandished a rusty blade hidden within his textbook, deftly moved it from his left to his right, and menacingly trudged out of the classroom, much like Jaggu dada from the slums. He then joined his gang, who was watching this unfold, and began hurling the crudest, vilest slurs at Pandu and his mother. These were accompanied by a variety of vulgar gestures.

Pandu seethed with a potent mixture of anger and sadness. He wanted to beat every one of them within an inch of their lives. Images of triumph, where he was soundly trashing them, flooded his mind. And then he realized: he was an orphan, more or less. His father was no more, and Lakhu's father – well, like it had happened during their last fight, he would hit Pandu's mother, attempt to disrobe her. The rage that had surged through his blood evaporated, and a wave of exhaustion hit him.

Lakhu–Bhaga's bored gang of goons saw that he wasn't coming out and responding to them in kind. So, they resorted to calling him 'impotent' and 'girly' before leaving.

Pandu saw that Lakhu–Bhaga were at a safe distance from him and exited the class, picking up his books. They felt heavier than before. As he entered the slum, he noticed that Lakhu–Bhaga were engaged in a game of marbles near the chawl. The courage he'd mustered up to that point quickly vanished. The fear of an impending fight made him turn around and circle the perimeter to find a different way in. He entered his house, heart pounding. He frantically waited for his mother, or, God forbid, Lakhu–Bhaga to come. A lot of time went by, but nobody came for him. He felt liberated. His fear receded. This was when he realized that he'd been famished since the morning. He sat in front of the stove, and as he pulled the *bhakri* basket towards him, a few cockroaches fell out. This made his hair stand on end. He took the plate that was kept near the stove. Then, he picked up the pot that was lying in the stove's ash heap and upturned it on the plate. A mass of fish fell out noisily, his plate now full of offal that had a sour stench. Sheer disgust flooded him. His chest swelled and tightened painfully.

His mother was not who she used to be. Not like before. She did not arrive early yesterday, despite him waiting for so long. And when she did arrive, she didn't say a word – just got to work. She somehow put together a meal consisting of bread and a vegetable, and, laughing and smiling to herself, went off to sleep. Didn't say 'eat'. Or 'have some more'. This morning was no different. She'd risen early, had a bath and was sitting in front of the mirror, clad in her newest sari. She always held the mirror near her face. Or let the sari fall from one of her shoulders, revealing a silver chain and a new necklace, made of gold. She kept fidgeting with these, adjusting their position. She caressed her breasts. Pulled at the hem of her sari. Untied and re-tied the knots of her blouse.

Thinking about her antics in front of the mirror made him feel extremely anxious. There was a hysteria-filled abyss in his stomach. Perhaps she had kept the foreman on the hook after all? His heart pounded again. He had no desire to eat. He threw the plate, got up and resorted to his usual method of dealing with anxiety: immersing himself in his studies in front of the door with his slate, board and bag in tow. But he couldn't focus. He kept thinking about the names he would be called by the boys, or the others in the slums. To avoid this slander, he thought about leaving his house and running away for good. He felt like throwing himself to the ground and weeping. But then, other women would notice and continue insulting his mother, so he kept the tears at bay. He also kept invoking her name in the hope that she would arrive soon.

He tried looking for her in the crowd that was now returning home. Suddenly, Dagdu's figure appeared and staggered towards him. Stood right before him. He spat contemptuously and kept mumbling as he kept him squarely in his gaze, even as he was walking away.

'Fucking whore! You've left your child behind, and now you're going shopping with your new man, isn't that right? If money was all you wanted, you could've just called me! For so many years, I've itched for you, wanted you, but now, you…'

He let loose a steady stream of profanities and kept walking. Pandu's very being felt like it was aflame. As usual, thoughts of murder assailed his mind like thunderbolts, destroying his innocence with every strike. He was overcome by the urge to take a colossal rock and smash it into the stumbling Dagdu's skull. His mind was tinctured by the shade of red that would pour forth when the rock hit Dagdu. His body quaked with a ferocity that accompanied those feelings of revenge and frustration. The meaning behind Dagdu's mumbling took the form of bullets that penetrated his heart. But then, the spite, rage and vengefulness that he felt for Dagdu vanished. These feelings were now directed towards his mother instead. Each question that arose in his mind pushed him further into the maw of anguish… *Is that why she's always late? Is that why she was late last night? And what will happen to me now? Who will feed me?*

He had many questions, questions that made him cry. 'Mother!' he said and threw himself to the floor. He stifled his mouth to prevent the neighbouring women from hearing his sobs. But one of his neighbours did hear, and when she did, she yelled, 'Oh, look, Chandra's mother – look over there. That's that bitch's spawn sobbing, see? Go take a look and find out what's the matter, will you…'

'What?'

A few women from the houses nearby stepped outside. They saw him and expressed their sympathies while berating his mother in the same breath.

Meanwhile, his mother was hurrying home, worried that he might be starving. But when she saw the gaggle of villainesses in front of her house, her yearning to see him faded. The evidence before her made her think that he had finally joined her enemies' ranks. He now resembled his father, who had been her foe, her adversary. She rapidly walked towards him, her anger giving her movements a beautiful, bewitching quality – which the entirety of the chawl was riveted by. Years and years of labour had had no effect on her lustrous, fair skin, her shapely frame and alluring gait. Dagdu's wife, who possessed an elephant's build, an elephant's colour and an elephant's teeth was incensed by her and she screeched at her husband, 'Why are you lot just staring, eh? This wench is just smearing her shit all over! Give her a nice kick in her waist, I say!'

Pandu's mother was inflamed at this indirect insult, but she held her head high.

'Oh, you W-H-O-R-E!' Dagdu, itching for a fight, pretended to sneeze while berating her. Pandu's mother heard this but kept moving, emboldened by the foreman's backing. Dagdu, looking at her graceful movements, spat, 'Tch, you… go fuck yourself!'

Dagdu's wife saw the lust in her husband's eyes, but she let out a placative laugh. The women under her sway covered their faces with the hems of their saris and joined in, turning their necks as they hee-hawed. Dagdu was suddenly irked by the sight of his wife's disgusting teeth that had revealed themselves in this bout of laughter. She saw him getting angry and immediately covered her mouth as she continued to hurl insults at Pandu's mother.

Pandu heard all the commotion and momentarily forgot his anguish. He sat up and peered outside. He saw the liveliness in his mother's movements. Her chest proudly thrust forward, her neck raised high, the new, spotless, impeccably worn sari on her body, and unexpectedly, her lips stained by the deep red of betel juice – he saw all of this and validated her enemies' belief: she was immoral. And so, he left her side and mingled with the enemy instead.

She saw her son scrutinize her from head to toe, his gaze suspicious. With that, whatever affection she had left was reduced to ash by an inferno, fuelled by her fury. Suspicion had turned her consumptive husband into Satan, and she was convinced that her son was as fiendish as he'd been. Their gazes were one and the same. Those evil eyes painfully reminded her of the physical and psychological atrocities that she'd suffered.

Like Pandu, his father used to sit in the doorway when she returned from a day of toil. As soon as he would see her, the poisonous snake of suspicion would slither in his eyes. The fact that she was loyal, the mother of his child, or that she was slaving away to save her ailing husband – none of these things mattered. She was a villainess. He thought that she earned her money not by virtue of honest work but by selling her body. After all, who would let a beauty like her go unmolested? Rather, why would she resist these base urges? When she reached the threshold of their home, he would look at her legs, her thighs, the sari covering her thighs, its folds, her stomach, breasts, blouse, hair, lips, cheeks – everything. And as he took every pore in, his distrustful eyes would meet hers, constantly looking for signs of sin. The slightest change in her expression would enrage him, and he'd ask, 'Your sari seems very, very loose today. Those knots… they're tied too quickly. Too messy, they are. Did someone fuck you, eh? Whore! Let me see… Let. Me. See!

He would eventually look at the wad of notes tucked into her sari's waistline. If there was no money there, he'd ask, 'You servicing men for free? Is that it?' Then, he would make her strip. Scrutinize every little atom on her belly, her breasts, her back. If he happened to see so much as a little scratch from an inconsequential itch, he would start chastising her.

'You vixen. Trying to trick me? You won't complain even if you don't get to eat. But your addiction to… *that*… that's what caused me to be this way. I'm dying. A "consumptive". But your lust couldn't be sated, could it? And now you'll sleep, without a care in the world!'

He hit her to cripple her, mar her beauty and take it away. And so he repeatedly assaulted her mouth, nose, forehead and eyes. If she endured his beatings, then he would tell her about his sinister plots to murder her in her sleep and horribly impair her young, supple body. Frustrated by his madness, she'd told him, 'We'll go back to our village. The people here harass me. You're harassing me, too! There, it's different… the water's clean, the air's pure. There's money to be made. As for brother-in-law, he'll forget and forgive. No quarrel's too big. There, our boy's sure to grow strong, and fast.'

'The village? And just because I've turned into this husk, you've remembered that pig? Oh, you villainess, I'll die. I'll die and kill you and that boy, but I'll never take HIS help!'

'That pig' was a reference to his elder brother. Her husband had hit him with an axe because he thought he'd looked at his wife lustfully. From then on, they had distanced themselves and lived like exiles. They'd looked for work from this village to the next, but everywhere they went, he'd doubt any man that crossed their path, get into fights and get beaten. Eventually, they reached Mumbai. Beat and be beaten – that was his way. After a particularly nasty fight, he contracted tuberculosis. As the disease eroded him bit by bit, his lust drove him insane. He tortured her. Tried to eradicate her youthfulness, her beauty, her vigour.

Once, she was fast asleep after a hard day's work. The smell of bibba woke her up. Her husband was boiling the seeds. Her child was nowhere to be seen. And he had disrobed her entirely. *What is he going to do to my body?* This thought plagued her to the extent that she began wishing for his death. She started having intercourse with him more frequently. Even when he didn't want to, she'd beg him for sex. All to end his life. After a few days, right before her naked form, he died – emaciated and utterly sapped. She believed that she had killed him. In the village, there were many proclamations regarding her behaviour, her inadequacies, her wickedness. Condemned, she endured hellish torture and suffering for the last decade. Dagdu's wife and her cronies ganged up on her and beat her too often. They'd strip her of her sari. Men would gleefully rush to beat her and touch her at the slightest provocation. Once, Dagdu tried raping her in front of all the slum dwellers. The torrent of abuse, suffering and pain seemed unending.

Her son's gaze, laden with suspicion, made her recall every painful incident. Her mind was no longer in the human realm – it had entered the realm of ghosts, monsters and demons. Violence was its creed. Shaking with rage, she stood in front of her son, intending to purge his blood of the filth his father had bestowed him with – filth that caused him to look at her with those eyes.

Dagdu – whom she wanted to brutally murder, and whose death she kept envisaging every single day – coarsely spat, 'Thoo! Fuck you! Even your boy doesn't know who you are any more!'

'And how will he know? His eyes are all fogged up!'

'But that foreman, he's a strong fellow, isn't he?'

'Oh, that he is, ha ha, he is!'

At this, Dagdu's wife muttered something that sent shivers throughout her body.

Her rage peaked, and for a moment, there was only darkness before her eyes. If there had been a sickle, an axe or even a sizeable stone within her reach, she would have killed Dagdu, his wife and the helpless, frightened boy sitting at their feet before ending her own life. But there was nothing. No weapon in her hands. She rushed inside, and her voice sounded like a thunderclap when she responded to Dagdu, 'You bloody pimp.

You're nothing but a dead man walking. May your mouth rot! You'll become a leper, and your limbs will wither to dust… You, torture me? Oh, you'll die. You're forgetting that you were beaten within an inch of your life. And you'll be thrashed again. Mark my words, you'll be beaten today.'

As she was going to utter the foreman's name, she stopped and shifted her focus from Dagdu. She looked at Pandu instead and assailed him. 'Die. Just die like this. Your old man kicked the bucket just like this, quivering and snivelling. You pimp, if your father heard anyone insult me like this, he'd lose his mind. But look at you, you pansy! The fuckers that give me trouble, gut them with a bloody knife, you hear! Snatch their wives and daughters! I raised you with my own sweat and blood, didn't I?! Then snatch their women! And if you can't manage that much, then run off with your tail between your legs! Get up! Get. Up!'

Her thundering voice only served to confirm Pandu's belief: his mother did not need him after all. She'd kill him, just like she'd killed his father. He had to leave. He stood up but was so overcome by emotion that he broke down. He covered his face with the hem of his shirt and continued to sob uncontrollably.

The sound of Pandu's cries quelled her anger. His concave, sunken stomach, skeletal limbs, his protruding ribs and the pallor of death that had overtaken his body – she took all of this in, and her rage subsided. A wave of motherly love washed over her. A terrible question sliced through her mind: *Does my son also have tuberculosis?* She was scared and looked at him with regret in her eyes.

'Hey, do you cough, too? Do you retch and puke? Are you getting feverish during the day? *Arrey*, baba… tell me… tell me. Why do you torment me like this?'

Before she knew it, her eyes were overflowing with tears. Her heart was torn with doubt. She quickly rose to her feet, took her son inside, went to the stove, looked for a match, clumsily struck it and lit the lamp. With frightened eyes, she scanned Pandu's body for any signs of tuberculosis.

'Say something, my sweet… Tell me, do you get a fever at night?'

He didn't answer. He wanted to stop crying and begin looking for a way out of the house. But he couldn't stop. On the other hand, she grappled with this sinister doubt that grew with every passing moment. The reason was simple – for the last month, since she'd fallen in love with the foreman, her attention had shifted. Since then, she hadn't even touched her son. Her desires, suppressed for over a decade, had finally been set free. The foreman occupied every corner of her mind. Because of this, she didn't have it in her to go near Pandu or to hold him close. She thought of how to explain all this to him. At that moment, she caught sight of the clothes that she'd bought him. With great determination, she tried keeping a level tone and said, 'Son, forgive me. Look, I got you a pair of trousers and a soft cotton shirt. Go on, remove your old clothes. Wear these instead. And sit down to eat! Forgive this stupid woman. You'll forgive me, right? Say something. Anything.'

He calmed down at the sound of her tear-struck, sorrowful voice and looked at the clothes. She'd brought him two sets, and there were two sets for her, too – saris and blouses. But this sight made him remember last year's Diwali.

Last year, during Diwali, he'd had an enjoyable hot water bath and was all cleaned up before wearing the new pair of clothes she'd bought for him. He walked around with a spring in his step. His new clothes and his creamy Brahmin-like skin made him an instant object of envy for the sweaty Bhaga, who was clad in soiled clothes. He spitefully asked, 'Pandya, you bastard. You seem to be having fun! When did you get a new pair of clothes? Who gave these to you eh?'

'My mum.'

Lakhu's father, Dagdu, looked at the widow's son strutting around and was quick to comment, '*Arrey* Bhaga, he doesn't need to worry about anything! Her business is doing quite well, you see? So many customers! Every one of them must be spending at least five or ten bucks!'

The adults in the vicinity cackled noisily at that. A hurt Pandu stung back venomously, 'Tell your mum, too. There'll be many customers. Like the crowd at a fireworks store.'

This blow managed to get under Dagdu's skin, and he started to beat him. Pandu yelled. The people nearby tried to separate them, and Pandu's mother, who heard his yells, rushed to the scene. She flew at Dagdu to free her son from his clutches. In response, Dagdu let go of him and grabbed her instead. Like an enraged animal, he began wringing her neck. Hitting her. Tearing her blouse. He shoved his body into hers a few times, then threw her against the ground and started to disrobe her. He had straddled her when Pandu slammed the biggest rock he could carry on his head. Livid, Dagdu took after him, intending to beat him senseless. After all that, people finally came in the way and ended the fight.

Since that day, Pandu didn't wear new clothes. He was reminded of Dagdu's words as he looked at the set his mother had just purchased: *He doesn't need to worry about anything! Her business is doing quite well, you see?*

He'd warmed up to her and moved closer to her. But this made him stop. He had the same image of her as the others did. Now, there was no point in staying here. Here and at school, every single day, people would tease and beat him up. He had to run. These thoughts caused his blood to stir, and his legs seemed to carry him out of the house of their own will.

'Look. Just wear these clothes. Sit down and eat.'

She pretended not to notice the shift in his gaze and rose to pull him closer.

'Make your corpse wear them! You whore!' he spluttered in rage and stormed out of the house.

'Pandu!'

His blow, caused by a weapon that he had never raised against her before, destroyed her. Her anguish was immeasurable. She stood there in the doorway, looking at his retreating back.

'Endure the punishment of your sins!' A voice erupted in her mind… and in the minds of those gathered around. She collapsed to the floor. Looked outside as the sadness took over her and wept as she wondered about him and his fate.

Time passed by. The night lengthened. Fearing Dagdu, she'd closed the door and waited for Pandu with her back to it. But he hadn't come. Suspicion gnawed away at her. She muttered incessantly to herself, as if reciting a litany of her sins in the presence of God.

'…Look, my child, you left me, thinking of me as immoral, unchaste. You've saddened me more than your father ever could. You, your father and everyone else in the slum have harassed me beyond compare. I endured a lot – too much, perhaps, for both of you. When your father died, Mohammed Mistry wanted to marry me and even pledged his scooter to me if I agreed. Walji Seth would repeatedly send twenty-rupee notes, using Thaku Mama as his messenger. This Dagdya was ready to put all of his service fund in my name! Despite all that, I slaved away for your sake. But you… since you became old enough to understand, you stopped talking to me. Distancing yourself from me. Started believing what people said about me. Last Diwali, Dagdya tried to rape me. If only you saw me as a mother, then I wouldn't seek any other relationship. I would have your support. But you left me…'

She started crying. The room felt like a cemetery to her. She was lonely and fearful of what Dagdu might do, so she latched the door. Then, she thought, *I've locked the door and alienated my son forever. Even if he shows up, he might not come in*. She was restless, torn between standing and unlatching the door and sitting where she was, keeping it latched out of fear. That was when she heard a dog bark – roughly from the same direction where Pandu had run. She thought that perhaps he must've returned and quickly got up, removed the latch and said, 'Come, my child, please forgive this sinner.'

A few seconds later, the door swung open.

'Come, child!' she said.

The thick-limbed, brawny foreman stood at the door. She was tongue-tied, silenced by her mistaken anticipation.

'What happened? Why did you get so scared? Why are you shivering?' He drew her close. Under the pretence of wiping away the sweat from her forehead, he began caressing her cheeks, neck, breasts and back.

The veena of desire slowly strummed within her tormented, unsated body – an emotion that had been repressed for the last decade. She lovingly clung on to it.

She didn't hear her son's voice calling out to her – nor did she hear the knock on her door. Thinking that his mother must have slept off, crying to herself, Pandu pushed at the door, calling out to her. On seeing her in the foreman's arms, his saddened conscience was torn asunder. He was immediately reminded of the other slum dwellers who stood outside the door, and his heart pounded with shame. He fled, and she promptly freed herself from the foreman's loving embrace to give chase. But he had run off and was too far. The foreman pulled her back heartlessly. Pandu ran as if he were running for his very life. The dogs in the slum ran after him, and as he realized that he was being chased, he ran even faster, crying and yelling as he tried to escape. People emerged from every last house in the slum. She vainly tried breaking away from the foreman's clutches, but she couldn't escape – as if stuck in quicksand…

मैदानातील माणसे

The People in the Field

The pale field near the powerhouse was, yet again, experiencing the famous serenity of winter. The cold, like an invisible axe in the sky, blindly assailed the people of the field. It seeped through every single one of their pores. And those homeless, jobless people, not having the financial or mental resources to build a simple hut, were seething with jealousy while eyeing each other's warm blankets. Husband and wife clutched and pulled at the blanket as they yelled and fought each other for it. Children wailed for their parents, and the dogs wriggled, trying to infuse their bodies with some warmth.

The wind rampaged through the field like an enraged elephant and trampled everyone underfoot. But there was an exception. The wind merely caressed David, who was anything but hapless or weak, a distinct contrast to those people. It injected his battered body with life force.

Coated in blood, he was sprawled in the bushes under a gigantic, black, leafless tree. His assailants had tossed his knife near him. He made a living by collecting protection money from the slum's liquor distillers and their companions – the shopkeepers who supplied the distillers with raw materials. Tired of his ever-increasing demands and unbearable beatings, they had conspired with the police to beat him within an inch of his life, and, thinking him dead, had left him lying in those bushes near the field. The cold wind slowly revived him. He endured his numerous pains and managed to stumble towards the trunk of this tree. He couldn't bear to take another step, so he sat right there. He rested his gigantic, brawny back against the tree and placed his feet on a platform that jutted from above the trunk. The bloodied locks on his head, hardened because of the blood, framed his fair face. Despite being utterly beaten, his neck remained upright. His enormous chest, an affirmation of humanity and godliness alike, easily weathered the cold gusts of wind. His craggy hands, generously huge and full of vigour, gripped the knife and his laid-back form contained the strength and pride of a tiger. Like the waters of the Ganges wash away sins, the wind washed away his exhaustion, restoring the temperament that made him either godly or satanic by the virtue (or vice) of dishing out pain – depending on the context.

At the same time, the cold was causing utter chaos as it dashed against the powerless people of the field. It was especially, stupendously cruel to the tuberculosis-inflicted Abdul Karim. Lacking any proper employment, he donated blood for money so that he could sate the addictions that had been plaguing him since his younger years. He had become penniless after having spent all his money on prostitutes and *qawwali* nights. Like Chandi, the cold danced thump-thump on his skeletal frame, and he thrashed around like a rooster whose neck had been twisted, ready for slaughter. Pain erupted from his fingers, his toes and his vacuous insides as his blood froze and clotted, and he violently shrieked, slamming his feet and hands against the ground. Sometimes, he hunched over so that the cold did not assail his chest and his stomach, and at other times, tried burying himself under the earth as if getting under the comfort of a warm blanket. However, the earth wasn't embracing him or hiding him, but rather leaving him wide open, and the cold kept pouncing on him ravenously. Given all of this, he thrashed around for dear life, screaming, 'Oh, Allah, just let me live… let me live, have mercy…'

But Allah wasn't hearing his prayers. Wasn't granting him mercy. As if that wasn't enough, even the people around him remained motionless. They didn't lift a finger to pull him away from death's gaping maw because, like him, they had been destroyed by the cold. Near him, there was an old couple, Zhunkavu–Supad, who had fallen asleep under their filthy blanket. Scattered around them was all kinds of salvage material – paper, glass, asbestos – shoved in unsavoury gunnysacks. They'd obtained this after scrounging around all day in the Chembur waste pit, intending to sell it off. The two of them had but one soiled blanket, and like Abdul, it had given up in the face of this bone-chilling cold. Despite having been together for their whole lives, the couple warred for a larger share of the blanket the moment their bones quivered. Supad, who possessed a fiery temper, who had been chased out of his village, his job and a chawl in Mumbai and who would smoke copious amounts of ganja to forget his woes, was beating his wife, and Zhunkavu, who had endured his beatings was exasperated, fighting him to stave off the cold. She stubbornly clung to the blanket and fended him off. Angered, she painfully reminded the old man of all the wrongs he'd committed against her, and he returned the favour by heaping a torrent of abuses (and the occasional strike) with his knee or elbow. His hold on the blanket was as strong as ever.

With his head resting on a sheaf of trashed newspapers, a khaki-coloured sheet of paper for a mattress and a sack for a bed sheet, the sixteen-year-old Ramu lay near them, shivering. His knuckles were white from tightly gripping a sack full of paper. For the last four to five years – since his parents had passed away – he had been eking out a living by collecting scrap paper from garbage bins on Mumbai's streets. The cold assailed him, too, but he held on to the papers for dear life, fearing that someone might snatch his precious wares away and burn them for a moment's warmth. He held on to the sack despite the shooting pains in his limbs and his fingers, desperately trying to remain vigilant, lest someone break open his skull with a rock as he slept and make off with his bounty. There was no one near him who could possibly harm him, but the cold made him unable to see the good in others.

Beyond him lay a monstrous, hulking Tamilian leper under a tattered blanket with a puppy in his arms. The pup whimpered constantly, and he kept pulling it close. The cold whipped him, making him shiver, and he yearned for his rotund, fleshy wife. Deprived of the pleasure of her company, which he'd enjoyed for ten long years, he was intensely restless. In his delirium, he thought that he held a woman in his arms, and he would caress the pup – sometimes with affection, and at other times, with the frustration that accompanies a nagging suspicion that one's wife has been sleeping around. He hugged the puppy tight, and when it would whine, he would talk to it, consoling it. He was frustrated by the fact that his married life had come to an end.

At a small distance from this leper, in a clearing amidst a clump of bushes, was a spot usually occupied by another homeless couple. A week or so ago, the husband had been nabbed by the police as he begged on the roads. They had let her go because she was pregnant. She lay there in that spot after having begged all day for some morsels of food, and the ever-increasing cold made her stomach ache. She was unable to tell where this pain came from – pregnancy or the cold. She would yell periodically. There was a gang of Phase Pardhis, a tribe nearby who, despite hearing her cries, were determined to ignore her. The cold had utterly defeated them. Their children were wailing, fighting for a blanket, and because it was illegal to build a fire so close to a power station, their parents tried a variety of things to keep warm. Other couples embraced each other, some slept over each other, some engaged in sex, and the wind, this enemy of humanity, would occasionally blow so hard that it would leave them bereft of whatever clothing they had left and expose them to its cruelty.

Kunwar Soni, who lay between the grandmother and grandfather of this gang, was torn apart by the maddening lust that this cold had kindled in her. She wriggled restlessly, and her grandparents were irritated by her incessant movements. They told her to stop squirming, to be silent. But deep inside her, the storm that had been set in motion was not to be quelled. It would not let her stop and made her remove the blanket from over her head, compelling her to look at the amorous couples in her gang engaged in various acts of lovemaking, and they, without too many clothes to shield them, engaged in intercourse as it gave them warmth like nothing else could. Looking at them excited her. There was a crazed glint in her eyes. The cold made her forget her grandparents' threats. Tired of her behaviour, her grandfather shooed her off and embraced her grandmother tightly for warmth. The dazed Soni, who was now at their feet, shivered even more as her eyes darted back and forth, from the consorting couples to her tightly embracing grandparents.

Her grandfather rasped a command, 'Don't just sit like that. Sleep behind me. Hold me tightly.'

She did as she was told and held him close. The warm touch of her youthful, tender body immediately made him feel better. He began caressing the old woman. The chill in his bones lessened, and the faded sense of desire in his body returned. Then, he yelled at her and told her to get up. As soon as she did that, the old woman told her to lie behind her instead – and she kept switching positions in this way, sometimes behind him, sometimes behind her. They kept using Soni's young body as an aegis against the cold, sapping her strength. She was colder than ever. After a while, she walked away from them and lay down, drawing a thin, tattered sheet over herself. The couple continued their sexual activities, and her restlessness increased as she continued observing them. She wanted a young man to lie next to her, for him to rub his hardened body against hers, for him to caress her. She had distanced herself from her grandparents for this very reason. She wished that someone would come to her – but no one came because the younger men in her gang were all her cousins.

Wave upon wave of cold washed over her, twisting the hunger she felt into an ugly obsession. She would lie down, ashamed, and periodically sit up, looking at those under the blankets as they pleasured each other. She was delirious as the cold and the lascivious acts around her intensified. Her intent to sin sharpened. She got to her feet – all she wanted was to huddle inside a blanket with someone, anyone. In the distance, she saw the monstrous leper, Ramu, with his sacks of paper next to him, and Abdul, who was thrashing around because of the cold. Just as she was thinking about who was the best choice between them, a voice called out to her. She saw a man making gestures at her, telling her to come close. She scrutinized him, saw his thick, warm blanket and determinedly took two steps in his direction before stopping. The cold had frozen all her veins and muscles. She swiftly moved forward and stood before him. The man cast his eyes on this girl, infused by the tenderness of youth, before forcefully embracing her. He then sat down with her still in his arms and engulfed the two of them in his blanket.

Meanwhile, David, still resting against the tree, was witnessing the plight of these people. The spectacle of Abdul writhing under the cold's torment twisted his heart into knots. The sounds made by the pregnant woman in that clump of bushes made him shiver involuntarily. The tragic tale, woven together by the fights between Zhunkavu–Supad, the old couple, made his colossal hand tremble with the urge to do something, and the sight of Soni, who had to sate a stranger's lust for an iota of warmth under his blanket, completely numbed his brain. Lost in these thoughts, he puffed on one cigarette after another. After some time, he could hear the Phase Pardhis clamouring, 'Where is Soni? Where is she?' Her grandparents roamed around the field, leaving many inhabitants temporarily bereft of their blankets as they checked for her whereabouts. When they finally saw her with a stranger, having given up her chastity for his blanket, they started to hit them both. Their assault was merciless and unending, with other gang members, both young and old, picking up whatever they could find and throwing it at them. The man was drenched in his own blood and eventually fell to the ground. These people – ordinarily not cruel – were deriving warmth from their violent labours. The rekindling of their flame of life made them completely ignore their victims.

Their vile behaviour incensed David to the point where he yelled out in sheer frustration, 'Hey! You Pardhis, leave him… Are you going to leave him or not?'

Gripping the knife in his hands, he leapt like a cheetah from his spot and made a beeline for them. The Pardhis heard the fire in his voice, looked at his aggressive, determined gait and feared for their lives. A single glance at his knife made them flee in all directions, and the women and children went so far as to wail and cry out for help. He looked at their cowardly actions and turned his back on them. His eyes, which had acquired a certain ugliness that comes with the threat of violence, took in the sight of the ailing Abdul Karim – who was periodically raising his back and throwing himself to the ground. He abruptly stooped, grabbed Abdul by a fistful of his hair to make him look upwards and asked, 'And who might you be?'

His thunderous, heated voice and touch startled the already frightened Abdul, who spluttered,

'I'm a poet… For my whole life, I have only loved women and poetry… and all I got in return was punishment…'

'Meaning?'

'Please don't hit me. Your merciless world has already killed me. Let Allah witness my death so that he never sends me back into this world. Let me go.'

Upon hearing those words, David's grip loosened. Abdul fell back to the ground. This bout of violence made him bellow, whimper and cry in pain. In between these bouts of anguish, he fervently took the Lord's name. His melancholic outburst created a conflagration of both heat and tears in David's mind. His gigantic hand slipped back into his pocket. There was nothing but a box of cigarettes in there. His heated gaze travelled across their surroundings in a bid to help Abdul and settled on the sack atop Ramu's chest and the cartons scattered around the old couple. He ran towards Ramu first, who had been alerted by Abdul's wailing, and was clutching at his paper-sack livelihood with renewed vigour. David was incensed at Ramu, who was clinging to something that would barely make him any money at the expense of another young man's life! Ramu tightened his grip even further when he saw David approach. He begged for mercy.

'Brother, please don't take this. Don't step on an orphan's livelihood. What will I eat tomorrow? Take what you need from those old hags!' He was trembling, crying, talking and tightly clutching his sack, all at the same time. This insistence, and the force with which he held on to his possessions, wounded the hurt David. Looking at a beggarly weakling like Ramu trying to fight against him, annoyed him no end. These feelings made him snatch the sack, empty it and cover Abdul with it. Then, he walked towards the papers that had spilt out of the sack, lit a match and set them on fire while yelling, 'Warmth! Warmth!'

The sack, combined with the heat from the fire, made Abdul feel better while also giving him hope that perhaps he wouldn't die today after all. But Ramu's distressed speech rang clearly in his ears and made him want to throw off the sack covering him. However, David's powerful presence ensured that he couldn't muster enough courage for it – and David was looking right at the woeful Ramu. His disposition, which made him care for those weaker than him, was now wounded by Ramu's pitiable words. He was in deep thought about how to alleviate Ramu's pain.

David's statuesque, unmoving pose began to worry Abdul even more. Supad–Zhunkavu, the old couple, was just waiting for David to leave when suddenly the beggar woman in the bushes screamed with all her might. It was a sound that often comes with the process of bringing a new life into this world. David, on hearing this sound, vibrated like a delicate string that's just been roughly strummed. He moved away, trying to locate the source of that voice, and as soon as he was at a safe distance, Supad–Zhunkavu took the opportunity to get closer to the fire and enjoy its warmth. They picked up those papers – practically the remains of Ramu's scattered livelihood – and threw them into the fire to keep it going. Ramu saw their evil actions and was so inflamed that he felt like breaking open their skulls with a rock, which he now started looking for. His frenzied eyes darted around fervently.

While he looked for a sizeable rock, the old couple continued warming themselves. The pregnant beggar continued screaming, and every scream hastened David's blind movement in her direction. Each step pained him. The cold wind caused volcanoes to erupt in his wounds. But he kept moving, gripping the knife with sheer fury.

The hapless first-time mother hesitated in shame because now, even as her child was about to come into this world, a tall, menacing man was speedily moving towards her. Her body's unusual position made her extremely uncomfortable. The pace of her childbirth was in disarray. With the desire to liberate herself from suffering, while also being concerned for her child, she anxiously yelled, 'Hey! Don't come this way. Turn back, turn back…'

The concern and stiffness in her voice managed to slow him down. He stopped, and at the next moment, furiously retorted, 'You whore, who the fuck are you to stop me? Speak to me like that again, and I'll break your face…' He moved forward and caught a glimpse of the red mass that lay between her thighs. Afflicted by a mixture of fear and disgust, he stepped back, shut his eyes and turned around, shivering as he walked away. A few steps later, he realized that he hadn't helped her at all and stopped. He was deep in thought. But for the life of him, he couldn't think about how to help her. He opened his eyes, thinking he ought to look elsewhere for help. Instead, he was treated to a ghastly vision that drove all those thoughts right out of his head.

The old couple's desire for warmth had reached its peak. They were snatching away the last bits of Ramu's papers and hitting him mercilessly, raining blows on his face, his neck. With every blow, their temperament became crueller. David instinctively ran to bring this old couple – who'd turned into demons because of the cold – to their senses. The trio's brawl was turning fatal with every step he took towards them. The cold had angered the old couple to such an extent that they were completely unaffected by David and the threat he posed to them. In fact, they hastened their efforts to snatch Ramu's papers and burn them, hitting him with all four hands. To avoid getting knocked down by any of them, as he had been before, he trampled all those who were in his path. His victims thrashed about, then froze once they saw the naked blade in his hands. By that time, the old couple had triumphed over Ramu and successfully snatched the last of his scraps in addition to the cardboard sheet that he was using to cover himself. They turned to the fire with their spoils and were about to burn them. Ramu quickly picked up a large rock and hurled it, hitting the old woman squarely in the back of her head. The blow downed her, and she collapsed. Instead of seeing if she was all right, the old man focused his attention on Ramu. Seeing the murderous glint in his eyes, Ramu scurried backwards and stood where he was, a stone in each hand.

If the old man had so much as moved an inch forward, the cowardly Ramu would've shredded his head and his face. He was that angry, that scared. David, knowing the extent to which a cowardly man could go when cornered, and not wanting a kid like Ramu to rot in prison like he had, roared with a surprising amount of compassion in his voice, 'Ay, boy, throw, throw those rocks down. Now, are you going to put them down, or should I thrash you?'

Scared, Ramu immediately tossed them away and looked at the old woman, bracing himself for the old man's attack. Her eyes were red, bloody. Her headscarf and clothes were caked in blood and were turning redder still. Looking at all that blood, Ramu turned towards David and began crying profusely. David felt like embracing the innocent, orphaned child and stroking his head. He surged forward with his arms wide open, like Christ, and a tender, pristine sound rang through the air, reaching his ears… 'Aaaaaa… Whaaaa…'

His subconscious was stirred at the sound of a baby innocently crying, and the urge to see that tender face, like a red flower in bloom, prevented him from reaching Ramu. The cries pulled him back. The anxiety in his mind amplified. He instantly lowered his arms and stood like an antelope; his ear pricked to hear the baby's sweet, honeyed cries. Despite waiting for a while, he didn't hear its cries again. His mind, utterly stupefied at the sight of the people of the field and their inhumane behaviour, began exploding in doubt... *Why does the child not cry? Did his mother, under the spell of the cold, gulp him down hungrily like a beast – no, a cat? Did she attempt to destroy the only evidence of her sins?*

This doubt unsettled him, and he turned his back on Ramu. He walked around aimlessly. Ramu, thinking that his troubles would somewhat lessen if he entered David's embrace, sadly watched him go with a pitiable gaze. David, meanwhile, wished to prevent something far more unfortunate from happening, like the mother intending for a cruel fate for her child because of the cold, or, God forbid, killing the child out of sheer desperation. Consumed by this humane urge, he pulled off the blankets from those in his path, searching for the mother and her child. The people being uncovered and left bare rose, incensed, but one look at the menacing knife in his hand or the movements he made with his brawny physique was enough to make them grind their teeth in frustration and back off. David, meanwhile, walked all over the field ecstatically, yelling in an intoxicated voice, 'Get up! The woman has delivered a child... it is time for Christ's birth...'

He was completely unaware of what he was saying or doing at that point. He screamed, pulled off people's blankets, slung them over his shoulder and trampled every person under his thundering feet, causing chaos throughout the field. Eventually, he encountered the massive Tamilian leper. The man was occupied with the puppy, thinking of it as his curvaceous wife and kissing it with fervent affection. David rudely interrupted him, stripped him of his foul-smelling blanket while trampling him underfoot and moving forward.

His spoilt mood, the cold's mercilessness and the impact of a boot trampling his rotting foot – all these things made the leper insane with fury. He stood, picked up the grindstone that served as a pillow for him, muttered a vile curse and rushed at David.

David spun around. He wasn't used to such an insignificant man itching to fight him, let alone tolerating abuses hurled at his mother. He steadied the lethal knife, easily capable of slicing a man from right to left and met the leper's challenge. The leper hesitated and fell back as he saw the promise of death flash in David's eyes. Nausea gripped David's mind at the sight of the leper's deformed face, and the thought of sinking his knife in his tainted blood disgusted him. He lowered the knife, contemptuously spat and turned around.

The leper looked at David's elephantine gait, his large, sculpted physique and was consumed by jealousy. David's contempt made him want to kill him. The last straw was when David threw off the blankets he'd slung on his shoulder to the ground. He gripped the grindstone that was still in his hands and brought it down on David's head. Having lost a lot of blood because of the beating he'd received in the morning and having remained upright by sheer force of will, David finally fell. The people of the field, who'd lost their humanity because of the cold, swarmed and assaulted him. They took perverse pleasure from this act as it also warmed them.

David, who had remained as untouchable as the naked flame despite having lived a violent life, was beaten by the people of the field. He bled, prone on the floor, reddened like the muddy idol of a god. Every one of his assailants, on the other hand, bared their cruel excitement by scrapping and howling at each other like dogs, trying to salvage their decrepit clothes, saris and blankets from the pile David had just discarded. And the pregnant woman in the thicket dug the earth with a sharp stone to dispose of the bloodied bundle, the clothes and the umbilical cord, and the cold intensified, fuelling the malice that lay deep within the hearts of the people in the field, lifting them from humanity itself…

शिक्षण

Education

We uttered slogans of satyagraha as we streamed into the jail. The jail woke with a start. The political prisoners before us added to our sloganeering from their respective barracks. The next few minutes were engulfed by the clamour that ensued. When the din died down, a tall, fair man who had completely shaved his head approached me and asked, rather intimately, 'Prabhakar, *arrey*, since when did you become a leader?'

Over the last two to four days, I had been influenced by the heady, protest-heavy environment to the point where I'd become a sociable, vigorous defender of the public – so I assumed that this stranger had somehow heard about me. I didn't give a second thought as to why he sounded so familiar, so I simply greeted him with great enthusiasm, asking, 'Brother, when did all of you arrive? How many of your batches are here?' I didn't even bother getting a response before rapidly and consecutively hurling a few choice slogans, like tridents in the whirlpool of sounds. There were no bounds to my excitement and my volume. We'd converted the jail's stony silence into a joyful, festive cacophony.

After the enthusiasm for proclamations died down, I told my aide, 'Gangurde, it is time for you to take the lead.'

'Yes, leader, I shall prime the cannons.' And he took over.

Just then, the young prisoner embraced my hands and asked, 'Prabhakar Pagare, what is this protest about?'

'This is a protest organized by the National Republican Party for landless labourers, and I'm the leader of the one-thousand-and-fifty-first regiment!'

'Which means you are a leader after all – but then again, you were always a leader. In high school, you'd given Tavkar sir a fabulously fitting reply, that too on Gandhi's birthday. Tavkar had said to you, "Pagare, pick up the broom," to which you replied, "We have swept the streets for five thousand years. Gandhi aspired to become like us – you should, too."'

I still hadn't recognized this prisoner who held my hand with such familiarity and who also knew intimate details about my school life. But the excitement around us prevented me from clarifying his identity in a more direct way. For the sake of it, I said to him, 'College is shut for the holidays. I was fed up of sitting at home and twiddling my thumbs. So, I told my father, "I'm tired of wasting my time here. I'll participate in a protest and then go to jail." My father was one step ahead. He instantly retorted with, "Go but be careful. Our government is more trigger-happy than the British ever were!" To which I said, "They might be, but I won't die. I still have much to learn, have to obtain an MA, PhD, get married and produce some dozen-ten-dozen children that can piss on your dhoti!" My father laughed heartily at that. He called out to Mother, "Hope you're hearing what your son has to say!" She replied, "I heard that just fine. His tongue is just as sharp as yours. Yesterday, I told him, 'If you're bored, then just go to Pune to your uncle's.' He tells me, 'That Suki, she keeps hovering around me like a dragonfly. And my aunt keeps insisting on me getting married.'" "So what?" my father asked her, fully intending to provoke a response. I, too, added, "Father, I would've married her. But her nose, at least, should've been sizeable – at least as much as a biggish button." My dad snorted with laughter again. My mother, feigning anger, told me, "Just get lost, and tone down that rudeness!" So, with great respect, I bowed to her, joined the protestors (who were waiting for yours truly) and sloganeered loudly to the point where it would reach her ears! She yelled back, "Don't scream so much; your throat will get strained." Then, we broke curfew and reached here. We'll stay for fifteen days or so… How did you get here?'

'I murdered someone.'

'Murdered someone!' The calm, collected voice with which he uttered these terrible words sent shivers down my spine. I wondered how exactly this murderous young man knew me. I was already regretting the familiarity with which I'd spoken to him earlier. One of the protestors, who'd managed to listen in on our conversation, grabbed my arm and pulled me away, saying, 'Oh, look there! The second regiment has arrived.'

More sloganeering could be heard from the outside. We matched it from within. Some time went by like this. Despite all this, the fair young prisoner had not moved an inch. When our voices died down, he asked, 'It's not what it looks like. What I meant to say was, I'm here because I was accused of murdering my brother-in-law. They threw me in jail because there were other pieces of evidence that attested to my rotten character – evidence of chronic drunkenness, unruly behaviour and even assault. Personally, even I was tired of the outside world. Was there no end to the violence? My sister had already taken her own life. My mother had forgotten the concept of sorrow and enmity and I… I also will die. Maybe tuberculosis will take me. All those beatings have destroyed my joints. Every bone aches. There's really nothing to live for. I approached you because I saw a dear school friend of mine – spoke to you because I could not help myself.'

His speech affected me. I took his hand in mine, trying to remember who he was. Suddenly, the fog, which had accumulated for seven-eight years now, dissipated as a ray of light burst through it. I realized who he was. I realized that he was a timid, mute boy with a delicate demeanour – an artist, a friend, brimming with intelligence. He was Lakshman Jadhav. I asked him, 'Lakshman, you have a murder charge on you? Your brother-in-law's?' As the questions issued from my mouth, my memory returned.

Back in high school, he had the fairest skin of all the boys. He was handsome, could draw extremely well and was proficient at his studies. He wanted to become a lawyer because his widowed mother kept reminding him that it was his father's dying wish. He'd become a high school favourite in his first year itself. His artistic talent had been noticed and praised at the school's annual function. When he was in his second year, his one and only sister got married. Many of the children and teachers were stupefied when they saw how beautiful his mother and sister were. After the wedding, his sister moved to her in-laws', and a shadow fell on his fair face. He turned into a complete introvert, where the sorrow that lay heavy on his heart was quite apparent to those around him. This was when he and I became friends. He took the lead when it came to cultivating this friendship – and soon, we were inseparable. I started frequenting his house more often, and those visits revealed the source of his angst. It was his sister's extraordinary beauty and his highly attractive mother's widowhood.

A ruffian, who was from the same chawl where they stayed, used to bang on their doors at random hours of the night and call out to his mother. He also had a habit of spreading vile rumours to defame her. Her attractiveness, her ability to earn a modest income, and their house, which was in a slightly better state than the rest, all contributed towards this animosity that many in the chawl already felt for her. Her son-in-law made things worse. He was cruel and extremely insecure. Not a moment went by when he wasn't suspicious of her, and to keep her under his commanding influence, he would often beat her. Witnessing the beatings inflicted upon his delicate sister, his weak, timid and soft mind would quake with sheer frustration and rage. The power to set his brother-in-law straight was something he simply didn't have. His mother, in an attempt to placate her son-in-law, started giving him money. Most of her money was being spent on her daughter's household. However, these handouts only amplified his drinking – and with that, so did the beatings. Sometimes, he would send her back to her own house, utterly bloodied and bruised, and Lakshman would seethe as she recounted her horrific tales.

One day, he lustily put his hands on his mother-in-law while drunk. Since then, she vowed to not give him a single paisa. This enraged him, and after that, his drunken insults were often directed at her. He tarnished her reputation within the chawl and its occupants. This fuelled their enemies and made them bolder than before. Lakshman Jadhav's tender mind was being destroyed, bit by bit. Lakshman, who would usually discuss studies or create vivid, miraculous art in his notebook, now spent all his time fantasizing about his brother-in-law and narrating the horrific ways in which he would murder him. Perhaps he would kill him in his sleep or follow him as he swayed drunkenly on the road, throw petrol on him and set him on fire or hammer nails in his sinful eyes as they exploded – he would describe these sickening scenarios in great detail for hours on end. Those who heard him would shiver involuntarily, and more than his brother-in-law, it was he who became the object of fear among the others.

Sometimes, he would get restless for days on end because of what his brother-in-law had done to either his mother as he abused her or his sister, who he'd beat within an inch of her life. His face would become gaunt, as if afflicted by a great illness, and fever would set in. His weight decreased, and his mind seemed numb. I could not bear to see him like this, so I would divert his attention with books or keep telling him something – anything else, really. In this fashion, the second year went by. He'd barely managed to pass. Either that, or the school had intervened and given him a passing grade. After the summer holidays, we returned as third-year students. He returned, too. But this time, he looked sapped – like arid wood. His eyes had sunken into his skull and his mouth was lifeless, like a corpse's. Everyone asked him about what had happened to him. What made him change this much?

I, too, asked him these questions as I walked home with him. He gave me the same answer he'd given everyone else, but

I didn't think that was the truth. When I dug deeper, he finally admitted, 'I'm experiencing wet dreams.'

I asked him, 'What do you see in your dreams?'

My question caused him to break down and cry profusely. When his tears subsided, he muttered a slew of abuses under his breath like a madman. These were directed at his brother-in-law. His anger surged. His words were heated, and they singed me as I mutely listened on. After some more time, I asked, 'Weren't you going to tell me what you see in your dreams?'

'How can I tell you? It is sinful. Horribly shameful…' His tears returned. 'How can I tell you…' he managed to say.

'We might be able to look for a solution.'

'Really?'

'Yes.'

'Promise me you won't tell this to anybody else? Swear on the goddess of knowledge – swear on your mother and your sister.'

I dutifully swore an oath. He narrated his tale, his voice full of fright and hesitation, saying, 'The abuses that my brother-in-law hurls at my mother, at my sister – I see them. I see them as vivid shapes and forms. I cannot bear to keep witnessing such things. I feel like pricking my eyes, eyes that show me such sinful visions, even in my dreams. I feel like going up to the terrace and jumping off it. I see my mother, naked, with my brother-in-law – my sister, too…'

His eyes had welled up again. Frustrated, he continued, 'I think that I will never get any peace unless I end that demon's life. Or… I should just leave my mother and sister and run away. Go somewhere else.'

I'd grasped his state of mind with such intensity that it warped my own. I fell into a state of melancholy, as if I was the one facing these cruel, dangerous trials. I thought, *If this continues, this multi-talented boy will turn into a madman. Or commit suicide.* I told him, 'Will you come and stay at my place?'

'It would've been my pleasure. But that swine spawn isn't beneath committing all kinds of heinous acts if he finds my mother all by herself. Give me some way to overwhelm him.'

'Go to the gym. That might help you take your mind off things, especially those dreams of yours. I read this in a book called *Swami Shivanand's Key Mantra*. Maybe you should read it too.'

'I, too, feel like exercising. But the gym is full of local thugs and hooligans. Knifemen. What if I become like them, or God forbid, my brother-in-law pays one of them to shank me? How will I eventually fulfil my father's dying wish?'

'No. That won't happen. Just don't let anyone else know that you're training.'

Eventually, he began training. In a matter of days, you could see the difference in his disposition and his movements. However, the sincerity with which he used to attend school diminished. Six months went by. He missed class more frequently. Sometimes, a band of wastrels would come and pick him up after school. The thick bonds of our friendship started thinning. Every now and then, he would avoid me. I, too, did not make any intense attempts to call out or talk to him.

Two to three months passed, and he failed his semester exams. After that, one fine day, he came up to me of his own accord, telling me, 'Yesterday, early in the morning, my brother-in-law beat my sister senseless. Her head was bleeding, and blood had thickly congealed around her shoulders. Her face was swollen. Even her eyelids refused to flutter. When

I saw the way he'd beaten her, I vowed that I'd beat him just like this. I will break open his skull, his face. My mother and I took her to the hospital. A police case was registered. The cops showed up and arrested him. He stayed there for barely a day before getting out on bail, after which he got drunk and returned home. Since I knew he'd come back, I asked many of my friends to help me deal with him. After some convincing, two of them agreed, and the three of us made a beeline for my house. As soon as we reached, I saw that he had already stained my mother's honour. Her sari was torn. His hand was in her underwear. The hem of her sari had been stretched and pulled at viciously. He was dragging her around by her hair, like an animal. A tug here and a pull there was all it took for her to collapse before being dragged off again. His knee drove into the small of her back as he told her, "Bring my wife back to me. Or you become my wife. I haven't sated my urges for the past couple of days. I'll only become a man now if I take you. Otherwise, my manhood will shrivel."

'And my mother kept pleading for her life, pleading for help from those around her. But no one did anything. My mother has never harmed anyone, and her behaviour? Immaculate, like snow. I saw her plight from a distance and fell upon him with a hockey stick in my hands with the intent to utterly defeat him. I hit him blindly, hit him anywhere and everywhere I could, but he was stronger than I was. Despite enduring my hits, he looked for ways to snatch the stick from my hands, and that's exactly what he did. Before he could sink it in my head, my companions fell upon him. He collapsed to the floor, unconscious. The hockey stick was still in his hands. We carried my mother away, and as we put some distance between ourselves and him, he got up and started running away. My friends prevented me from giving chase.

'By the evening, this news had fallen on my sister's ears, and she came to us and repeatedly prostrated herself before my mother, apologizing. After that, she went to her husband's house. As soon as he caught sight of her, he thrashed her brutally, like he wanted to take her very life. Their neighbours managed to extract her from his clutches. Someone tipped off the police. While he'd been passed out in a drunken stupor, my sister's mangled body was found under a car. She'd committed suicide.

'And in the morning, after I'd performed her last rites, I made a vow. Just like he'd slowly, surely tormented my sister before killing her, I'd kill him the same way. Slowly, deliberately, I will take his life. Starting today, school is over. But you helped me a lot. I will never forget that!' He pressed my hands together, took my leave, and after all those days, he'd finally appeared before me in jail.

I asked, 'Did you kill that beast?'

'Yes.'

'Did you have to kill him?'

'No.'

'Then why did you do it?'

'I did not want to, but it happened nevertheless.'

'Meaning?'

'That's a long story, but well, I might as well tell you. After all, we might not see each other again after this. You study at a college, and I rot here, in jail. Don't think I'll live for too long either. So…' He pulled me away from the crowd and began narrating his tale.

'I didn't have the courage to murder him. Like you, I was a simple man. He twisted me. Corrupted me. Killing him meant having a certain strength in your body. Having mastery, skill. To obtain these things, I went to one of Mumbai's high-ranking gangsters in one of their many dens. This gangster was dressed in a crisply ironed, starched khadi kurta, a jacket and a tight-fitting dhoti. He was definitely drunk on moonshine. Around him, there were other khadi-attired men, and some two-three young boys like me, clad in woollen pants. I went inside, mustered all the courage I could, and said, "Please let me join you!" "What do you mean?" One of the gangster's henchmen responded. "I want to murder someone." "WHAT?" they all yelled, now. Then, the gangster himself said, "Whose murder? Mine, or his?" He gestured to one of his henchmen. "My brother-in-law's." "Is he your wife's brother or your sister's husband?" "The latter," I said. "What's he called?" I gave him a false name. "What did he do?" "He killed my sister. And groped my mother," I told them, keeping it as brief as possible. "And what did you do about it?" "I hit him with a hockey stick. But he's like an elephant." "Okay, then!" Four months went by, after which he formally let me join their gang, and instead of becoming a lawyer, I began training to be a thug instead. I stayed at the distillery. Refined alcohol. Supplied my customers with illicit goods in plastic bags – sometimes on a cycle or in a taxi. I took a few killing contracts. I fought. I broke open two labour strikes, and during this period, I spent about a year in custody. My leader used the police to condition me and give me a thrashing. Sometimes, I even went to jail in the place of some important people – and took the beatings intended for them. These events were extremely common, and I saw the walls of many prisons. After that, my job was to be an assassin's aide. I would carry the knife up to the point where the target was in sight and hand it to him. After the deed was done, I had to swiftly clean the knife and return it to my pocket. I observed him and learned from his experience: how he approached the target, how he took their lives, how he moved. Then, my own training started – with a dog—'

'A dog?'

'Yes. So, you tie a mass of knots to one end of a rope. Dangle this in front of a dog. When the dog stands on its hind legs to bite it, snick, you quickly slice. But my dagger would always get snagged in the rope, or the cut would be too shallow. This turned out to be pretty dangerous because at least twice, the dog turned on me and attempted to kill me instead. One of those encounters was so intense that I really, truly thought I'd die. One of the adepts in the gang told me to start smoking ganja. Ganja helps calm the mind. I started smoking it, and lo and behold! My strikes started getting cleaner. The dogs died, one by one. After that, I attacked a few people. Some of them survived, some died. And now the police, despite knowing my name, barely uttered it. I also picked up the art of wielding a blade. My reputation as a deadly, smart hitman grew; so much so that my brother-in-law, who'd been hounding me all this while, started touching my mother's feet! Called her "mother", too! He started visiting me, and whenever I'd see him, my hackles would rise. But he'd turned into my slave. Whenever my hand went into my pocket, his face would lose all its colour.

'One day, my friends and I were standing on the road, chatting. He came before us, joined his hands respectfully and said, "Please come home for dinner tonight. Mother is here, too. Meet your new sister. I've asked for chicken to be made. Please come."

'I was incensed when he mentioned this "new sister". He knew I'd be furious, which was probably why he was grovelling helplessly at my feet. My friends convinced me to accept, and I did. Besides, I hadn't seen my mother in over a month and felt like meeting her. I didn't carry my trusty knife, which I kept on my person for twenty-four hours of the day. What if my mind, which loathed him to the core, suddenly had some untoward ideas? So, I went to his place and waited as his new wife busied herself in the kitchen. We had salted liver to go with our alcohol. My mother joined his new wife and was helping her with the preparations. As I heard them talk, the memory of my delicate sister made me tear up. I tried suppressing this sudden urge to cry. But all I could think of was, if this swine would've behaved like this – if he would've treated my mother like a mother, then all this needless ruin – it wouldn't have happened! I would be in college. Both our households could've flourished. I would have fulfilled my father's dying wish, too – you know it all too well. I had cleared three grades in a single year, and despite having failed the final, I was extremely intelligent right up to my fourth year. My hands were skilled. I was so good-looking, and my mind was pure. Despite living in a chawl, swear words were alien to me. I did not indulge in mindless violence. Our parents raised us patiently, nurturing us like flowers. This fiend destroyed both of us, my sister and me. How much grief and pain had he inflicted on my mother? And for what? All because my mother was widowed at a very young age, because she was beautiful and because I was too young and my mind was too fragile. Because I was a coward. All these thoughts finally burst through, and I started crying profusely. And he, in his guttural, alcohol-laced voice, told me, "Don't cry, don't cry. Oh, come here, come and placate your brother. Mother, look at how our brother is behaving…" Both my mother and his wife stood in the doorway. My mother dabbed her eyes with the hem of her sari. Sadness and frustration fuelled the fire within me. With the flames of rage coursing through me, this idiot casually shoved my shoulders to draw my attention and pointed at the hockey stick that lay behind the cupboard, saying, "Look, that's your hockey stick!" "Mine?" I asked.

"'Yes, yes, it… you had hit me with it, initially. And with such force…" He started praising me, thinking I'd be stoked, but all I could now think of was the heartless slander and shame he'd inflicted on my mother. My head exploded, and my murderous hands unconsciously moved toward my pockets, searching, ready to give him a dog's death. He saw the shift in my behaviour and immediately called his wife over. She came out and quaked with fear the moment she caught sight of my face. He said, "Look, this is your sister… Hey, why are you so scared of your brother? Call him dada…" "She will NOT call me that!" "Why not? Aren't you her brother?" He was looking at her with an expression that seemed undecided between eating her up or gulping her down. His fiendish gaze was back, the same gaze that had been the cause of my sister's death. "How can I be her brother... She is my…" "What?" "Don't raise your voice! For a few months, she stayed with me, like a wife would. We shared a room!" I yelled, hysterically. "So now…this seems like what an animal would do!" "You fucking beast, you'd count ME within your kind?!" I ran towards the cupboard, and with the hockey stick, unleashed all the rage, the frustration that I'd built up over the years on his body. His skull split open, and an arc of blood sprayed out. He collapsed on the floor, dead! I really didn't want to kill him. But he died. Died the death he deserved.'

Suddenly, sloganeering could be heard outside the walls. Both of us did not speak another word after that.

मरण स्वस्त होत आहे

Death is Becoming Cheap

My poet friend, and I were at home. He lay flat on the mattress and fished out a piece of paper from his pockets, saying, 'I'll frame that text I'd written while we were eating into a poem, you can drag your short story forward…'

And I dragged it forward. Or tried to. But it refused to budge from its spot. I tore the papers and discarded them. Then, my friend told me, 'Even my poem isn't taking shape. *Saala*, let me read out the rough text that I've put down.

'This is Mumbai…

This Mumbai was the first to dream

Of freedom, and it is this Mumbai where the earliest glimpse of it was seen.

The technological age was birthed here, in Mumbai first

And it is this technological light that was, in ten directions cast…

…this city is extremely vast, gigantic, an epic in itself.

Mumbai's roads are the cantos of this epic…

The Gangetic descent of freedom occurred in Mumbai, and its pure waters surged across its streets, reaching every possible area… because these roads are drenched in the blood of martyrs, and like Shiva himself, this city has a dreadful form…

'How did you like it? Let me set these diamonds into poetic sockets. And give Marathi poetry a precious ornament.'

I stretched my legs on the table, saying, 'Then do it!' even as I titled my short story, 'Death is Becoming Cheap in Mumbai'.

'What did you write?'

'Death is Becoming Cheap in Mumbai.'

'Nice. Looks like your story will come together pretty easily.' And he began assembling his own poem. But he couldn't manage. He erased every line he wrote, and wrote another. And another. When the page filled up, he would tear it into pieces. Even I was frustrated. I'd become bored of spoiling more sheets of paper so I snapped, 'Come on, let's step out for a bit.'

'*Saali*, even my poem isn't taking shape. Thought I'd used all my strength to stuff it within my framework and shut the lid, but it still won't be contained. It's stubborn, like a sal tree. Let's go…'

Both of us stepped outside the *vasti* and reached the main road. One side of the road near the railway tracks was full of *paals*★ – stacked on top of each other. The other side had some shops, a bank and a school. I heard a voice near one of these *paals*, 'Master…'§

I looked at where the voice was coming from. Bhimu Kadam found his balance as he made his way towards me, saying, 'It's like brandy. Would you like some? I was just at it when I saw you – and called out to you. Let's go.'

★ Makeshift houses made of old, patchworked rags and wooden sticks, and look like a tent with both sides left open

§ Refers to teachers and intellectuals

'Not now. I've just eaten. Did your wife get it for you?'

'That damned woman is missing again, since yesterday. Don't think she'll come back soon this time. I beat her a lot. She would keep suspecting the Madrasi woman next door; before that, it was the *kerwa maniwaali** and before that, she even suspected that girl who was rotting and dying! Master, that last girl, she must be sixteen or seventeen years of age now, but she's rotten from the inside out. Looks like she's contracted leprosy… but still walks around swaying her hips… she rotted pretty well. She started early. Her mother's pretty much the same. Abandoned her young child and ran away with some butcher. Truth be told, Master, I don't even like women. What's down there anyway but skin and bones…

'Just like that, I committed murder back then and ruined my life beyond repair. Now, I'm just fed up and angry with both – alcohol and women. The moment I get some money, I make a beeline for the bottle. If not, there's always my packet of ganja. And as soon as she starts fighting with me, crying and prostrating herself before me, begins suspecting me – I go back to her. Get bored. Go back. Oh, look over there, there's that ghost staring right at you. *Saala*, someone will come. Drink it all up.'

He slipped back into his hut to finish drinking, and we looked at the girl who was staring at us. She was standing next to her rundown shack, composed entirely of old gunnysacks. Her eyes and mouth were swollen, her face was marked with red-black stains. Not even a proper sari covered her body. There was no telling if her stomach had any food within. She looked exhausted, wilted beyond belief.

---

* Woman selling sky-coloured gemstones

I muttered, 'God gave that poor soul such a terrible punishment at the tender age of seventeen! She took to prostitution to survive because her mother abandoned her. Rotted away. This is a bloody life sentence. But who inflicted it? Why? What was her crime? Let's go…'

We walked along the road and looked at the *paal*s. Every *paal* clung to the railway fencing in order to stand upright. They exceeded the fence's height by four-five feet. And those along the road simply merged with it. Stones were placed on jute ropes and bags that encircled the *paal*s to prevent them from flying away. Looking at those *paal*s – and specifically at Bhimu as he sat there drinking, my friend said, 'Seems like he's extremely distressed. Like he's eager to die. Do you know anything about him?'

'I do. His name's Bhimu Kadam. From Satara. From a Kshatriya–Maratha household. Some ancestor of his squandered all of their inherited wealth. After that, Bhimu was the sole successor to their name. But he committed murder.'

'Whose?'

'His wife's.'

'Why?'

'He was a wrestler back then. His renown had spread from village to village. The village would quake at the very sight of him, and he was respected by everyone, young or old. Like this, he slowly elevated his family's standing, helping their name emerge from the obscure darkness. Earning fame. And on seeing his rise, his generational enemy from the very same village started to take steps in order to destroy him – by casting a net around his wife. Infatuated by lust, she fell into his trap in a matter of months, blindly obeying his every command. The flames of gossip fanned throughout the village and burned him.

'One day, instead of going to the *akhada*, he went to his house with an axe and hacked down both his wife and his enemy as they lay together, naked. And he immediately went to the police station and confessed to everything.

'After getting out of jail, he was so depressed about life and death that he didn't feel like going back home. Didn't feel like getting a job. Began doing anything that came his way. He'd fill his belly, spend the remaining money on booze and sleep anywhere he could. He spent five years in this manner – like a piece of trash, fluttering in the wind, and finally, he found this woman living in a hut next to the Mahim Creek. She's a street sweeper from Kutch. You'd be taken aback if you saw her. Full-bodied, lissom. Fair of skin. Used to applying kohl in her eyes. And a cleaner of toilets for four-five families in the building. The provider of *haatbhatti** for those families. Very coquettish and brave. Five years later, Bhimu felt that he needed a wife. That's why he started to live with her. She, too, loved him so much that she'd earn and feed him. She'd endure the bouts of depression that he was often struck by. Endure his beatings. When in Bandra, he accepted a job from a friend of his to slaughter goats and sheep at an abattoir. His depression had changed him to the point where he slaughtered them with glee. After a few days, he could skin lambs deftly. Once, as he was putting the knife to a lamb's throat, its dying gaze met his, and he was immediately reminded of the look his wife gave him when he beat her. He could see her struggle

* Desi liquor

reflected in the lamb's eyes. And then, the testimony he'd given in court flickered to life like the glint of a sabre's blade in front of his eyes… "Sahib, for the past few generations, my lineage has been weakly lying in the darkness. I was elevating it. Earning a name. And if my wife had waited for a little while, if she had endured it for a little longer, she would've lived. But she began hacking away at my name, destroying my penance. Began eroding my humanity. And so, I rose and hacked at her, hacked at her arm. Now, I don't wish to live any more. Hang me…"'

'He said that?! Wah, wah. Beautiful! What happened after?'

'As soon as he recalled this memory, he started to slash the lamb in a frenzy, even as it kept trashing in a pool of its own blood. On seeing his murderous zeal, the rest of the butchers ran towards him, took the knife from his hands and calmed him down. He lost his job, and the owner took full repayment because he'd spoilt the meat and damaged his surroundings. After that, his bouts of depression became worse to the point where he wouldn't eat. Wouldn't sleep. He would simply sit in one spot and keep smoking ganja. That woman from Kutch would work. Bring him booze. Look for ways to bring him back to his senses. But the lethargy that would come with the cascading rain would never leave. He would be subjected to these terrible bouts every monsoon. Sometimes, he would simply be numb to everything that happened; otherwise, he would wreak havoc on his surroundings. At the same time, his hut near the Mahim Creek was washed away. He built another one with whatever little remained. The municipality razed that to the ground. And then, he came here with whatever was left. If this house breaks down, he'll perhaps build another. Or he won't. One of these days he'll simply end his life under a passing train – as casually as he smokes ganja or drinks!'

'And his wife – meaning the sweeper woman – will get herself another husband!' the poet friend said.

'She's already a step ahead. She goes and stays somewhere for eight-odd days. He doesn't say anything to her. Not because he's beyond redemption, or because he's some kind of pimp, but because he's saddened – like a sage. Living and survival have become one in his eyes. His mind is dead. Or perhaps his sorrow is something else entirely…'

'What a dreadful character. You should write your story on this. "Death is Dirt Cheap" is what you should name it.'

Suddenly, a train thundered past. Our gaze followed it. The train's light revealed a group of women near the railway tracks, their backs turned as they defecated with their *tumbrels** next to them. Both of us averted our gazes immediately out of shame. My poet friend, with his head still lowered, asked, 'Whose hut is that?'

'That's Ranu Nagvekar's. He's a tuberculosis patient. He has four children. His wife does housework in a few bungalows nearby, he shines shoes. But the other shoe-shiner children don't let him work in peace, and besides, if he begins coughing, his customers immediately put a handkerchief on their noses and get up, fearing infection. They leave. Some of them pay for whatever he's done until that point while others don't even do that much. It was because of him that I got to know more about this slum. When I couldn't focus at home, I came to this park and began writing. That was when I heard a commotion. On

* A makeshift pail made out of a used tin oil-can

seeing many people racing towards a shaking man, I followed them. And who should I see but Ranu Nagvekar clutching his chest, writhing on the ground in agony. He was drenched in sweat. When I enquired, I discovered that his wife was ill. In a bid to earn, he would reach for and grab the feet of any stranger who passed by and start polishing their shoes if they fell to the ground. In that vein, he'd gotten a hold of a person's shoes and was attempting to take them off when the man shook his leg violently. His kick caught Ranu squarely in the chest. So he lay there, writhing. A boy who looked like a well-dressed loafer was rubbing Ranu's chest. Another old, middle-class man was fanning him with his scarf and many others had formed a circle around the one doing the kicking. Some said he should be taken to the police. A doctor should be called. This man shouldn't get away. Hit him. A couple of them decided to beat him up. Others got involved. The attacker, meanwhile, was loudly declaring to everyone, "He isn't hurt! He's faking it! He's just doing this for money."

'But Ranu's writhing and thrashing had intensified. Red spittle pooled near his lips. The crowd saw this. All of them surged as one and turned against the youth, who, out of fear, gave Ranu a ten-rupee note. It took a lot of begging and pleading for him to get out of that situation.

'After that, when I met Ranu at the park, I sympathetically enquired about the whole incident. He told me, "When the youth said, *He's just doing this for money,* was when I decided to truly fake it. After that, I began thrashing my feet in a more exaggerated way. I got the money and my wife's illness was remedied. My children ate rice for eight days. Now, I grab people's feet in the hope that they'll actually kick me. But they don't do that. Don't give me five-ten rupees. And the cobbler's children don't let me work either. Prevent me from finding customers. They snatch customers the way a crow snatches worms. Dupe me. Tease me. Make me cry. I've become a plaything for those little demons. Just like a crow pecks at an ageing animal in an attempt to break its will – they do the same to me. Make me feel like life isn't worth living."

'Before all this, Ranu was a printer in a sari-printing shop and eked out a meagre existence on his salary. His mother died and left behind only debt, which simply piled on the debt he already had. As he was repaying this, he contracted tuberculosis. The owner fired him because he couldn't work. Other owners refused to give him a job. To avoid starvation, he took a *pagdi*★ for his house. Started living in a hut. The slum burnt down due to an illicit alcohol distillery, which led to the slum rehabilitation authority always being a step behind him, and now he's here. I'd asked him once, "Where will you stay during the monsoons?"

'He replied, "If I can raise some money, then here. If not, on the railway platform. If not, then in the shadow of a building that's being built. What are we but completely discarded people, we'll live like cats and dogs, live anywhere…"'

On hearing this my poet friend remarked, 'We are all people whose desires have been repressed. Their sorrow is so all-pervading that they cannot think of anything else. But if someone were to give them this realization, then…?'

'Then they… they would burn Rome!'

'Let's go! That uncle is calling out to us.' We left a few *paal*s behind as we walked.

★ Subletter

'Come, gentlemen, come!'

We stood near Chacha. My poet friend was looking at him with an incredulous expression on his face. The uncle's demeanour and appearance seemed regal, like a nawab's. The poet asked, 'Are you from a family of nawabs?'

'How so?'

'How is your nose so robustly large? All my aristocratic Muslim friends have a nose like yours.'

'What's that on your head? Why is your face, your head so swollen?' I asked Chacha.

'I'm just unlucky. Last night, I went towards the railway platforms to take a dump. My foot got stuck in one of the tracks and I fell. I don't know how long I was unconscious. Lost a lot of blood. Our Ramu *bhaiyya* – from *teenpatti* – arrived there for the same purpose as I had. Came closer to frisk my pockets. And then, as soon as he recognized me, got me here.'

'How are you now?'

'How do you think?' He showed us his bandaged feet.

'Where's Jalal?'

'Gone to the station to fetch water.'

'Okay. I'll swing by tomorrow.' I began taking my leave, knowing that Chacha always asked me for money.

'Do you have eight *annas* or so? I couldn't go to the market today.'

I gave him eight *annas* and we moved forward.

'What's his story?'

'I met him through the people of the slum dwellers' association. This Chacha was once a schoolteacher in Hyderabad. He knows Urdu and Farsi. He knows enough English to write formal applications. His children were in

Mumbai, so he leased his agricultural land and followed them. All three of his sons lost their way. One was completely useless. He would spend his time in the company of an entertainer – a prostitute. As long as the money remained, so did she. After that, he became her servant. The second son was addicted to drugs. And the third had a multitude of children from his two wives. He could not sustain them. His first wife died. The other died during childbirth. And the responsibility of all these children fell on the old man's shoulders. After a while, the son vanished, leaving him with the children. To feed these little demons, the old man sold off his house and took to the streets. The children who were old enough were sent off to work in restaurants or the houses of rich men so that at least their food was taken care of. Even then, two remained. With Bhendi Bazaar's slum-destroying police behind him and the children in front of him, he reached here, after having lived on this road or that one. It took him seven to eight years to make this transition. Eventually, the older children left. The youngest child now begs and brings food back. The old man eats. Chats people up. Sometimes, he goes to the market and does some accounting for people on a day-to-day basis. He can't see well and doesn't have the money to buy glasses. He takes a few *annas* from people like me for his *beedi-kadi*. And tries scaling the mountains of every day with Allah's name on his lips.'

'You write a story on this Chacha. "Death has Become Very Cheap". The daughter-in-law dies. Meaning, she dies due to this forced pregnancy. Ten children. Their father, who couldn't care less about whether they live or die. The old man does the same, and out of ten children, keeps the youngest one close. Doesn't care for that one either. It'll turn out very nicely. The children on the streets from the Gateway to this place – they'll at least get some attention. Write—'

'Look at her. The one in the satin ghagra, in the green bodice, in the sheer red *odhani*. Looks like she's full of life. Compared to the people we've seen so far, she's energetic. Her dark skin doesn't prevent her from catching your eye.' My poet friend kept looking at the woman selling sky-blue gemstones. She seemed sturdy and firm – like a statue carved out of onyx.

'Every morning, she steps out with a trunk and when evening arrives, she selects a man and brings him back. The trunk contains neem brushes, *kunku*, wax, needles, *kali poths*★, glass marbles, anklets for children, *bindlyas*§, sky-blue gemstones and hair-removal soapsuds. Sells sex. The man whom she brings to the hotel pays for her dinner, which she eats over there itself. In the morning, she gets up, washes her face and goes back to the hotel.'

'And this man hasn't even built a hut. Who is he?'

'This is Barku, who's from somewhere near my village. We're close. He's lame, so he's always sitting in that chair-shaped vehicle. He eats in that car, and like a bull, shits and pees wherever he sits. And like the virtuous wives often found in Hindu scriptures, his wife, Sharja, takes care of him like she would her own child. Back in the village, people call her *Satpativrata*† and she, too, calls herself exactly that! If she hadn't taken inspiration from noteworthy women in the Hindu Puranas, she would

---

★ A mangalsutra (necklace signifying marriage – often expensive and made of gold) made of black beads threaded together

§ Another word for bindi

† The ideal wife – literally, one who has vowed to protect and devote her life to her husband

never have stayed with Barku. Because he is crippled, sure, but he's an awful man. He used to work as a water carrier. He'd also dug many wells for work. He can hear the sound of water from within the Earth's womb. Can see it. One day, he was digging yet another well when the water suddenly surged all around him. He collapsed, and the force was such that he was permanently crippled. He'd often just lie on the mattress, prone. Like an animal, he started defecating right where he was. After a point, his father and brothers had had enough of his filthy behaviour. And then, they kicked him out of the house. Barku came to Mumbai with his wife and two children and began using them – particularly the eldest, attractive daughter – for prostitution, and started to hoard money.

'When he came to Mumbai, he had the same thoughts – motivated by jealousy and revenge – farmers from the village usually think like this. Defeating those who kicked him out, a separate farm, a big house, ordering his kids around like a king to work on the farm: these were his plans and motivations. He wanted to have more of a name in the village as compared to his hale and hearty brother, and he behaved in the way he thought was prudent so that his dreams could be fulfilled.

'When he first came to Mumbai, for the first eight-odd months or so, his family stayed together. And they managed to earn two hundred to two hundred and fifty rupees. And because there was some semblance of decency, some sliver of the farmer's way left in him, he went back to the village during the monsoons. In the presence of witnesses, he left the money he had with a wealthy shopkeeper for safekeeping and returned as the monsoon was receding. This time, however, having observed the behaviour of other beggars and their families, he began splitting up his own family. His greed had him assign different spots to the women and children. His wife began sitting near the mouth of the railway station, pretending to be blind, with jaggery in her eyes and an infant on her lap. His son, taking after poor Brahmin children, sported a topknot, wore a sacred thread and applied a fragrant paste on his forehead as he started to sit outside a temple. Compared to the other dark-skinned children, he received a lot more money, fruits and sweets. And his daughter, having recently hit puberty, would wash her hands and face, neatly part her hair from the middle, energetically wear a skin-hugging sari and push her father's vehicle, accompanying him on the streets. Began laughing at the men who openly stared at her breasts, her face. Began joining her hands together, begging, even as she unhesitatingly made provocative gestures at the men. And her blood began to stir with the desire to do what she had been witnessing her parents doing since they came to Mumbai. And then, after a few days, she began doing exactly that. She would loan out her young body for sex, giving what she earned to her father.

'And Barku, blinded by the jealousy spurring him to defeat his brother, did not even realize how deep his family had sunk. Without any regard for them, he was swiping at whatever money he could get like a wounded tiger would. This went on for a few days until a day arrived when she placed not a little but a good thirty rupees in her father's palm and disappeared for a month with a man.

'She had changed drastically when she finally returned. She looked like a newly-wed who had returned from her reputable, well-to-do in-laws.' Her skin was supple, fair. Her hair was thick, replete with a black sheen. Her face had bloomed, like a flower. There was *kunku* on her forehead and she was wearing an expensive sari and blouse. Her parents were elated upon witnessing this Brahminical avatar of hers. Barku motioned for her to come close and kissed her forehead. And just as well – even if she hadn't gotten married, at least she'd found a good home where she could eat and dress well. This was a much better outcome as compared to rotting away here, his wife, Sarja thought. Despite that, with sadness in her heart, she asked, "Whose sari is that?"

"Hers!"

"You came to visit?"

"No. They threw me out!"

"Why?" Sarja asked, frightened.

"His wife was peeved. He kept me around because she hadn't returned for over three months. She found out. Came back with three of her brothers. They threw me out of the house. And now, I'm here."

'On hearing this, he felt good and Sarja felt bad. In the same fashion, the next three-four times, the daughter would hand her father some money before going and would spend ten-fifteen days before coming back. But the amenities that she had obtained in the first house were never to be found again. One of these men had even decided to sell her off on Foras Road. Because of this, she was afraid of going off with random strangers. Resumed her business from home base. However, she'd ask her customers, "Hey, will you take me away from here? Will you buy a house and stay with me, make me your wife?" But no one was ready to marry her. At best, they'd take her to Haji Malang or some such convenient spot. She was petrified by the thought of sleeping and staying again on the footpath, caked in dirt, of selling her body to any hoodlum at whatever price they quoted. She began to abhor the idea of being sexually approached and groped by men even as her parents indulged in each other like animals in the open. She did not have an iota of respect, love and fear for her parents now. When her father did not grant her wish to build another hut, she started to think of running away from them. Her younger brother felt the same way about their parents. He could not bear to suffer the sight of his father's shit-stained posterior, could not bear to smell the stench. Much like other boys, he sought to get away from his father. But like his sister, even he could not find a way.

'The monsoons arrived even as these thoughts occupied their minds. And Barku only took along his son and his waist pouch that was burdened with money as he left for the village. The daughter was left behind because she needed to earn, even during the monsoon. And for the first time ever, he also left his wife behind to ensure that the daughter didn't run away and splurge all her money. If he had taken his daughter with him, the fires in her heart would have been extinguished, but thinking that he hadn't taken her simply because of his greed for money, she waited for a chance to escape. With the arrival of the monsoon, she could not bear to sleep under the awnings or at the footsteps of hotels and shops, curled up like a stray animal under the cascading rain. She could not bear to quiver in the cold, staying awake all night when there was no shelter to be found. Time and again, the good life that she'd experienced for a month was crushing her under the whetstone of sorrow. Because of this, she would ask about where the men intended to take her – regardless of what they offered. She went with them only if she thought that the place was suitable. Not like before, when she would enter toilets or even go behind a bush while being paid chump change. And under the gushing rain, for three months, she longed for the pleasure she used to get on a bed, under the soft sheets and the rich, nourishing food she had eaten, and she longed for the man who had loved her like a wife and treated her with respect, making her weep profusely. In the end, these pleasant memories made her everyday life unbearable to the point where she gave fifty rupees to her mother, sold herself, and with the help of another man, made the nearby brothel her home. She fell deep into the abyss and never emerged again.

'After two months, Barku obtained a promissory note to the tune of fifteen hundred rupees. Now, all he needed to do was obtain two bullock carts and build a small house. When he returned to Mumbai and found his daughter missing, he immediately wrote to his brother. "My daughter died under the train. Don't come here. I'll return soon."

'And then, he burdened his son with the responsibility of obtaining his daughter's share of income. Every morning and evening, he would dress him up as a Brahmin and make him sit outside the temple. In between that, he told him to shine shoes. The son didn't listen to him and decided to only shine shoes – avoiding all other work. And slowly, wisely, he began drifting away from his father. Sometimes, he would come back to him, and sometimes, he would stay out. After one or two years, it was as if he never existed.

'But even when two of his mature, earning children had left him, his greed refused to go anywhere. His attention was now on his rapidly growing son. If he was crippled, then he would garner much more sympathy, which would get him more money, and for this, he began telling his wife to begin twisting his son's limbs. She didn't listen. Because of this, they would fight regularly. A few days went by like this, and then, she told him amidst bouts of tearful anguish, "The boy was abducted…" She would cry profusely, endlessly. But he wouldn't listen. And a horrific realization dawned upon her: one of these days, he would sell her, too.

'Coming to Mumbai and spending his life on the footpath had ruined his life to the point where he was impervious to sorrow. Because today or tomorrow, his shoe-shiner son would come back to him. He believed that he would have many more children. And it wasn't only this! A man had given away his daughter to him, and he had finally won the battle against his brother. The people in the Maharwada were giving him respect.

'Like this, a few summers passed. The hairs on his head were turning white, and his body would shiver involuntarily. He had three children during this period. Like his first daughter, his fourth, too, entered her marriageable years. Began drawing in lusty gazes. And for the sole purpose of earning a name, he decided to marry her off with a lot of pomp and ceremony. Despite knowing that both her character and her body would be violated, he didn't send her back to the village. Because he was sure to get a large sum of money for her looks, and then this girl was subjected to a horrible fate. With the intent of forcing themselves on that tender girl, some eight-ten men encircled her one day, and…'

As I was about to narrate that incident, the *paal* next to us shuddered as if a bomb had gone off inside and crumpled to the ground. Someone was screaming with all the force they could muster. No sooner did we try taking a look than a woman – like a shimmering snake with her glossy black skin, silver bangles on her arms and legs and a supple body – emerged, entirely naked, looking like she wanted to run for her life. Soon enough, two men with knives in their hands could be seen following her. They swooped to attack her, one after the other. The second man grabbed her hair and pulled her back in a flash. She howled for her life, and many people emerged from their huts. Bhimu was the first to arrive. He had an empty bottle in his hand. On seeing the crowd surge towards them, the murderous rapists leapt onto the railway tracks, began pelting people with stones and disappeared into the darkness. The crowd gathered around the crumpled hut.

The girl was lying face down on the road. Blood flowed from her wounds. Someone covered her with a cloth, and a few people managed to prop the *paal* back up. Upon entry, they found her husband groaning, lying in a puddle of his own blood. He had extensive, lethal injuries. They were going to rape the girl in her husband's presence. On seeing this entire incident, my poet friend was shaken to the core, and in an incredulously agonized tone, said, 'Let's go.'

The two of us kept walking. We were now near the station. There was a massive crowd near the station's water tap. People were fighting for water, and a policeman – in the hopes that he would nab a young, beautiful girl – was scolding the crowd with two-three goons from the station accompanying him. Chacha's grandson, Jalal, was slinking around like a cat in the same spot with too many vessels in his hand.

My friend said, 'I'll throw away whatever I've written and keep only a single line:

"This is Mumbai. Here, human eats human and death is becoming cheap…"'

मवाली
Ruffian

It was a derelict graveyard. Humans and corpses alike had stopped coming here. Its neglect had allowed an infestation of creepers and vines to take over. The grass had grown tall enough to reach a man's head. It was here that Girija brought any customers that she could get. She was solving the problems of feeding herself without paying rent anywhere else. Girija lived as a dutiful mother would, with a sense of pride.

And five ruffians, whose pride and honour had been reduced to nothing but dust by Basha Dada (twice!), had come to take refuge in this very graveyard. One of them, Columbus, was lying on a grave, squirming in pain. Lalya, Rafael and Kashinath were clinging to Columbus to support his frame. The tall, bony, sallow-skinned Peter sat on another grave, stroking his yellow, bald head, watching the rest of them with disdain.

Rubbing his palms on some *bhringraj* leaves, Rafael, crestfallen as he gazed upon Columbus and his grievous wounds, suddenly noticed what was written on the headstone of this grave.

Rose, you left me on this wretched Earth and reached heaven… How am I supposed to live here without you?

His gaze shifted from the words to Columbus, the regal Columbus who had turned black and blue because of the beating he'd received, and within the depths of his mind, he suddenly remembered Jesus – as he often would when in a drunken stupor. A stream of involuntary, sudden prayers coursed through Rafael's head.

'O God, Columbus is a true, bona fide hero. Hercules! To think you'd lay him low like this – I'm surprised at your actions. O Jesus, Columbus needs to stay young – forever. He has the nicest heart; the fact that you don't know this, despite residing in all our hearts, is surprising. God, you ended his power and prestige, that too at the hands of these simple people. And then, you let the police cart him off to jail. You let him get injured, but somehow, a simple man like me withstood their firing. You gave him tuberculosis. And today, you doled out a beating from a third-class man like Basha. Wrong! Are you God or an enemy? I will never place my faith in you. I'll take revenge. First Basha, then Shakya and then all of those bloody buggers...'

'Brother, hurry with the leaves. We should quickly get comrade Columbus back on his feet and make ourselves scarce. Otherwise, we'll be fucked again – hurryyy up!' Lalya glanced at the pensive Rafael before tearing off bits of his shirt to wrap Columbus's wounds. His lips and nose were swollen, a testament to the punches he'd endured. Water dripped from his reddened eyes.

Rafael rubbed the herbal paste on Columbus's wounds with a heavy heart. Kashinath rapidly bandaged those areas, forming a makeshift poultice. In an attempt to get Peter talking, he said, 'Brother Peter, those guys broke two of my front teeth – if we sue them, we should get some compensation… but I'll tell you a secret, they were already loose!'

No one laughed at that. The prayer circling around in Rafael's head flapped its wings and disappeared into oblivion, and the fires of frustration, anger and revenge took its place. Peter's long, horse-like face showed traces of contempt. Without saying a word, his gaze shifted from one person to another in the trio that was desperately trying to save Columbus's life. The sight of Columbus being taken care of made him wish that Basha's 'Surge' gang would bring knives, daggers and axes and first tear into Columbus and rip him apart. Then, sink a dagger into Rafael's large, rugged chest and twist it. Cut Lalya into pieces and let Kashinath go after making him sing a Sehgal song. As for him, they should shatter his head with an axe…

But his wishes remained unfulfilled; the Surge gang was nowhere in sight. Time was slipping by. Columbus continued to squirm, and Lalya was serving him without turning his neck, his movements resembling that of a medical assistant at a clinic. A thin rivulet of blood trickled down his head, temporarily slowing near his cheekbone and falling on a particular spot on his shirt, staining it. The bright red wound on his elbow prickled painfully. Tinnitus ravaged his ears. But he was so focused on Columbus's state that his own wounds did not affect him. After ensuring that he'd done everything he could, Lalya turned his attention towards Rafael and said, 'Brother, don't think now. Let's just mount a direct attack. A last stand.' Rafael could feel his injuries more acutely now, so he remained mum. Instead, it was Peter who responded. He seethed and boiled internally, saying, 'This isn't a possibility now. I have no energy. You are also finished, and our hero, Columbus, has now been rendered powerless like Hercules was.' After his speech, Peter contemptuously glanced at Columbus. The others did not like this at all.

'How do we take revenge? Do you have an idea?' Kashinath asked.

'Me? Well, we'll take revenge. But not the way you think. I will avenge Columbus. Lalya will avenge me, and Rafael will do the same for Lalya.'

'Meaning?' Lalya yelled. Columbus's eyes flickered open.

'Don't get angry. Just think about it. We're used to fighting with our hands... but now, we're old. Think about it.'

Lalya believed in Peter's intelligence and started mulling over his words. His ram-like head, conditioned after all those hits, still had the power to tear into a man's chest and knock him to the ground. His punches hit hard, too. But Vashya, or Basha as he was known, had numerous hitmen in his employ, and most of them had made quite a name for themselves during the riots. He'd built an empire on criminal activities like Illegal gambling, betting and the illicit alcohol trade, which had bestowed him with wealth and amenable policemen. How could he combat these ruthless, elite gangsters with just his fists and his head? Even though each one of them kept a knife, Columbus's reputation and the aura he radiated made it so that they never had to unsheathe them. His name was enough to strike fear in the hearts of many. The police had put this very same Columbus in jail numerous times within a span of four-five years. The same people who had been paying Columbus protection money had now banded together to usher Basha into the spotlight and destroy Columbus. Now, it was impossible to gain any wealth or prestige. How could this happen? He began thinking of a reason. But no answer came. Why did people start to hate Columbus? Why did they not fear him any more? He couldn't comprehend it. Peter was still looking at him. Then, he laughed, tauntingly, before asking, 'Did you get it finally? Please tell me.'

Peter's question confused him. It was hard for him to openly describe the infamy, the misfortune and the misery that had befallen him. His eyes, which had kept Peter's sallow visage in sight, shifted to Columbus. Columbus, who used to roam around with the disposition of a king, whose gait resembled a prideful lion's, who looked like a two-tonne sack of sugar, compact and immovable – the handsome Columbus – was now lying here, his face black and blue. His sharp nose was swollen. His rough beard was mangled by blood and dust. The hair framing his face was unkempt – just like any average scoundrel's. The clothes on his body were soiled, ragged. Anyone who looked at him now would hardly fear him – only pity and contempt remained.

Seeing Columbus like this made his heart swell with sorrow, and he recalled the image of a robust, proud Columbus twenty years ago when he'd been in his prime. Lalya must've been all of seventeen or eighteen years of age when his father kicked him out of the house. He roamed the streets without food or water and looked for a job. But no one wanted to hire him. He'd stopped before an Irani hotel because hunger wouldn't let him move another inch, and then, the fiery Columbus sauntered by amidst a hail of greetings. Columbus noticed Lalya and called him over with a single wag of his finger. He took him inside the hotel, fed him and gave him as much money as his hands would hold. Then, without another word, he turned around and walked off. With Lalya in tow, the duo reached Mary's club.

Columbus saw that Lalya was still following him and decided to keep him around. He would give him money when he needed it most, but he never admonished him or lectured him. Curse words and abuse were out of the question. Columbus was always melancholic, and alcohol was his constant companion. When inebriated, he would look so beautiful that Mary would lose her mind looking at him. And Susan would keep kissing him despite his anger, enduring his hits just to eventually take him back to her place.

Just like Mary and Susan, there were a great many women who attempted to make him theirs, but he was never enticed by their words and gestures. He never uttered an ill word against women, nor would he hear one directed at them. Mary had vowed to gift her house and estate to him, but he still hadn't married her – and unless she insisted many, many times, he would not spend the night with her.

Every memory of Columbus he had was beautiful. Larger than life. But he couldn't find an answer to Peter's question by reminiscing.

'So, any ideas yet?'

'No.'

'Well, you'll never get one.'

'Why?' Kashinath, Lalya and Rafael shouted in unison.

'Columbus was never a gangster – and he certainly was never like Vashya!'

Lalya's devotion was dented by this declaration. Enraged, he yelled, 'Baldie, what the fuck are you saying?'

Kashinath added, 'People were so scared of him! Like one should fear a lion – and rightfully so! The terror! Terrific!'

'Terrible terror, more like…'

'All right, but…' Peter sniggered for a moment before responding, 'How many fights did he actually involve himself with?'

'More than you, that's for sure!'

'But the number of fights Vashya has fought? Comrade Columbus never exceeded his count.'

'Because Vashya is simple and Columbus? *Royal*,' Lalya retorted. He was rather pleased with this response, too. But Peter was on fire, courtesy their fresh defeat. He vengefully responded, 'In this simple fact lies everything.'

'Meaning?'

'Columbus looks like a military chief of staff. He's tall, tough and possesses a lion's grace. His eyes contain terror, but his face is tranquil, loving, like Christ's. One blow, and his enemy is usually down. Women are enamoured by him, and he's never needed them. I, however, *need* them. I've never worked in a place where women were absent. I couldn't afford eight-hour sessions with prostitutes either. So, I came to Columbus. Obtained a lot of women and a lot of money – for free. Also gave some people a sound thrashing in the process, so—'

'Rascal!' Lalya swore.

'Listen, Columbus can be considered great, but he can never be considered a gangster.'

'But why?' Lalya was angry, and his voice was getting louder.

'I'll tell you.' Peter sat back. 'I told Columbus that he should start getting into smuggling alcohol, gambling and betting rings. Create a terrible gang. At that point, such lethal young men used to come to Columbus, but he didn't speak to them at all. Not one word. How would they stand that? Those people then went to Vashya instead. Vashya kept increasing his wealth, his power and we… if Columbus had established his own crew, none of this would've happened. We'd have won and ruled like kings! And we'd have had so many women… I haven't slept with a single woman for the past year and a half. Why…?'

'Bastard!' Lalya abused him, but Kashinath saw the point in Peter's complaints. Rafael went so far as to hold Columbus responsible for everything that had happened to them today. He was angry at Columbus and at himself.

Peter continued. 'Leave it. Columbus knows all of Goa's routes. Many times, I told him that we should get into smuggling goods. But he shot me down. Columbus was never a professional gangster but a freeloader. Full of pride. He never held anyone else in high esteem. He never needed you or me. But all of you needed him. What's more, he didn't even need himself! Otherwise, he'd never have encouraged Mary to marry another man. That fucker has become a *seth*, and Columbus—'

'Yes! This is real talk!' Rafael declared bitterly.

'Completely false!' Lalya responded, his voice laced with fury, and simultaneously, he was reminded of an incident that Columbus had sorrowfully narrated to him once.

Columbus had stopped going to Goa. This was because the Portuguese government had tortured, and eventually killed, his mother and his wife-to-be. The story went like this – he was a member of the Goan army, appointed as a chowkidar *on the border. He drew the attention of many girls even back then but did not like any of them. Then, he saw her – the one – and she was everything he wanted. They started spending time together. But one fateful night, as they lay in the fields, his superior officer discovered them and demanded that she spend a night with him. This superior was notorious for this – if he saw an attractive girl, he'd want her immediately.*

Columbus denied him. The officer abused him while trying to grab and pull her close. Columbus pounced. In the scuffle, before the officer could even reach for his weapon, Columbus quickly trained his gun on the officer's chest and emptied the clip. The officer perished and Columbus prevailed. He then fled to Mumbai. The government arrested his mother and his lover to get to him. A few days later, he learnt that they'd died inside a prison cell.

This incident shaped Columbus's personality into what it was today. Columbus was awake now, listening to everything. He wanted to say something to them, but the words wouldn't leave his lips. He mustered every single ounce of energy he had to shove them out but to no avail. Up until that point, there were only rare occasions where he'd let himself speak freely with them. Now, he felt like he wanted to narrate the epic life story that flooded his mind. But his senses, rendered feeble by the beatings, were powerless to quell the typhoon of emotions inside him. Restlessness took over. A pang of pain shot through his heart. Sweat pooled around his forehead. It was Peter who noticed his state. He stood up, leapt towards Columbus and said, 'Look, brother!'

Columbus struggled to sit up. A bead of blood threatened to spill from his lips. Peter moved forward and slid a hand behind his neck to help him. Before he could even prop him up, the bead of blood exploded and flew, splashing onto Peter's hand. The sudden feeling of hot blood made Peter flinch with disgust, and his hand slipped, causing Columbus to fall back on the grave in an unceremonious heap. His neck jerked painfully. Columbus shielded his eyes and assumed a serene pose. His lips were bloody, but he was feeling better. Lalya's heart trembled. Peter attempted to correct his mistake by taking his shirt off and wiping Columbus's bloodied mouth and fanning him. The guilt of a thousand crimes was visible on Peter's face, but Lalya thought he'd dropped Columbus intentionally, leading him to shout, 'Rascal, sir was hit very hard… If you've got the balls, then fight him fair and square!'

Peter retreated. 'It was a mistake. Please forgive me – all of you. Please don't abuse me.'

'What are we supposed to do then? *Saala*, we took all these pains, and you didn't even touch his body when we were getting out of there. Now, when he vomits blood, is when you remember your friendship? You did that on purpose, didn't you?'

'Silence!' Peter screamed.

'You bastard, you first!'

Thinking that Lalya would attack Peter, Kashinath attempted to placate both of them, saying, 'Brothers, please don't do this.'

Both fell silent, but the fire of resentment throbbed and burned in their hearts. Kashinath tried thinking of something to quell it but was at a loss. Suddenly, his gaze went to the church.

A fleshy woman stood there, her back against the wall. She had a man with her. Both were in the throes of lust. Thinking that this spectacle would distract and alleviate the tense situation between them, Kashinath told Peter, 'Peter, look… look at the church…'

All four of them now looked in that direction. The man had grabbed her and was holding her close.

This sight made the lascivious Peter ache with desire. He got to his feet and started slowly walking towards them. Looking at his pale, bony back, Kashinath thought he was staring at a fresh corpse that had just been dug up. Eager to see what this skeletal fiend would do now, he followed him. After a few moments, the sounds of a scuffle, someone being thrown to the ground. And a woman's scream tore through the air, making Columbus open his eyes. Rafael and Lalya got to their feet.

'*Arrey*, Rafael, catch that bitch… Meanwhile, I'll dispose of this bloody pimp… Kashinath, check his wallet.'

Columbus cleared his throat. When they turned around, he gestured to them. 'Bring them here.' The sight of Columbus awake and in charge made Lalya happy, but Rafael's mood soured. Both moved forward. The woman ran in their direction, but her legs froze as she saw two bloodied, tall, partially naked, menacing men standing in her way.

Kashinath and Peter returned with the man. They'd thrashed him with a vengeance. He was extremely young. He seemed inexperienced. His clothes were torn, and Peter's blows had bloodied his nose and lips.

'Come on!' Rafael said, stealing a glance at her protruding breasts and meaty thighs. But she didn't move. Instead, she started crying. Peter inched closer. He let go of one of the man's hands, and lost all control when he saw her neck, her back and her waist. He surged forward, clung to her and bit into her cheek with his large, serrated teeth. She let out a blood-curdling scream, her hands groping at her own cheek to feel if he'd actually bitten it off. Blood congealed in the spots where his teeth had made contact.

'Leave her!' Lalya yelled.

'I won't. You're telling me to leave her *now*? Foolish!'

'Dada is calling out to us.' Peter was groping her. She struggled to get out of his grip, and this sight enraged Lalya.

'I'm telling you to leave her!'

'No, never. She's a whore. What are you valuing her for, huh?'

'Nonsense!' Rafael's sister was a sex worker. She'd practically raised him. Even when she married an officer and moved to Myanmar, she regularly sent him money, clothes and other gifts. Peter's insulting tone, combined with this memory, angered Rafael. He stepped forward, grabbed Peter's pants, pulled him close and let fly a powerful punch. Peter, already maddened by lust, bared his teeth and punched him back while somehow also tugging at her and screaming, 'Leave her!'

'No. We have to bring her to Columbus.'

'Leave it, my man. Let me just satisfy myself for once.'

'No.' Lalya pulled her away while Peter struggled to pull her towards himself. Rafael was loosening Peter's grip by punching him repeatedly.

'Rafael, please, let me just grab her. Let me kiss her, just once.' Peter started begging like an addict looking for his fix, but Lalya and Rafael managed to pull her away. Dejected, he put both hands in his pockets, and like a wounded animal, gazed at her retreating, alluring back with fervent desire. This spectacle and Peter's forlorn, lustful words unsettled Kashinath, and he loosened his grip on the youth he'd been restraining.

The two of them finally got her to where Columbus was. Peter simmered for a moment before following them, and Kashinath, fearing that Peter would take some drastic measures to satiate his desires, decided to intervene. The youth, who'd been left unsupervised, seized this opportunity and ran. Columbus appraised the woman before him. Her face, and specifically her eyes, made Columbus think that he'd seen her before – but where? Ruminating, he asked her, 'What is your name?'

The sound of his hoarse, quivering voice saddened Lalya, but only for a moment before he flared up and realized that she was refusing to say anything, let alone answer Columbus's question. He gruffly heckled her. 'You idiot, tell him your name! Hurry up!'

A strange fear gripped her because Lalya, who'd rescued her from Peter's clutches, was now demanding her obedience. She whimpered, 'Kanchan.'

The doubt in Columbus's mind cleared instantly. He said, 'You're Girija, from Bhingarya's.' She was shocked because he'd not only correctly identified her name but also of the madam whom she'd worked under some eight-ten years ago. She looked at him closely.

'How did you come here?' Columbus asked.

She'd been extremely famous in the past. There used to be a line of men waiting just for her at Bhingarya's. Columbus had appeared before her just like that – a man waiting in line for his turn. He remembered that she'd been caked with sweat. Her skin had turned pale. He sat on a chair set before the bed. Her eyes looked spent, the product of hard labour. He looked into them, disturbed, concerned. She requested him, 'Please wait... my waist, neck and head feel like they're going to break. Feels like everything is reeling, need some air... let me drink some cold buttermilk, and then...'

She gulped it down, told her attendant to get some paan and wiped her sweat. She stretched and cracked her back. He gazed at her lustrous, black, taut body. Her attendant arrived with the paan. She put it in her mouth and chewed it in a trance-like state, before spitting it out. Then, in a crestfallen voice, she said, 'Come.'

'Wait! Bhingare, how many people are left?' he asked the madam.

'Four.'

'Here, take fifty rupees. And she will be spending the night with me.'

He handed her the money, left and slept with another woman. He was her regular. After that, he never visited a brothel again. He still remembered those eyes – the eyes that stared at him now. He told Lalya, 'Let her go!'

'But she didn't answer yet! So, how did you get here?'

'A kind customer helped me run away. I had to run because I had a child. Now, I work as a maid at a bungalow owned by a Parsi couple, and in the evenings, I ply my trade on the streets. My boy has grown now, so how can I do my business in front of him? How do I sustain two lives with my paltry salary of thirty rupees?'

'Go!'

She heard Columbus's command, and her eagerness to escape the clutches of these demonic figures amplified. She instantly turned around. Lalya was angry because she hadn't even bothered to thank Columbus, and Rafael's blood stirred as he drank in the sight of her shapely body. He remembered Peter's criticisms regarding Columbus and was irritated by the hold he had on them. He wanted to stop her and defy Columbus, but the words wouldn't leave his mouth. His mind was dead set against Columbus's generosity. She'd barely taken two steps before Peter jumped on her, drew her close and bit her lips like a goat yanking the leaves off a tree branch. She collapsed under his weight. Peter's animalistic urges took over him as he saw her bend over, and he started obscenely thrusting against her. Columbus saw his fiendish behaviour and bellowed, 'Leave her!'

Columbus's voice didn't reach Peter's ears. He was rapidly, filthily trying to extract any pleasure that he could from her body, tearing through her like a starving dog would a fresh morsel of meat. His brutishness and the fact that he dared defy Columbus's orders was something Lalya couldn't bear. He snarled and landed two quick punches in Peter's side, turned him around and punched him a third time – squarely in the face. Peter fell to the ground, clutching at his sides. He remained there for a moment before rising, unsheathing his knife and assailing Lalya.

'Hold him!' Columbus stumbled and unsteadily got to his feet. Peter sliced, his knife cutting through Lalya's shoulder, its trajectory threatening to bifurcate his sides. But Columbus kicked the vulnerable spots on his legs from the back, causing him to fall again. Peter rose again. This time, from the way he rushed him, it was clear that he'd quite forgotten Columbus's generosity and greatness. He struck the hapless, recently resuscitated Columbus in his chest, withdrew the knife in a flash and made a beeline for Lalya. The somewhat neutral Rafael saw Columbus fall to the ground, picked up a stone too large for anybody's hands and lobbed it in Peter's direction. Peter's knife, meanwhile, found its mark in the approaching Lalya's chest, and before it could be withdrawn, Rafael's stone hit his yellowing, bald head, cleaving it in two. The stone, Peter and Lalya all seemed to collapse at the same time.

Kashinath saw these three firmly steer themselves on the path to certain death within mere seconds and was mortified beyond comprehension. Somehow, he sympathized with Peter the most. He'd personally seen the effects of what happened when an unsatisfied man and woman came together in a moment of blind, unbridled lust. He also didn't think that there was anything wrong with that. To think that Lalya would hit him in his sides and Columbus, in a bid to end him, would target the weak spots on his feet, and then, Rafael, would deal the final blow with a skull-shattering stone… Had Peter committed such grave sins to deserve these fatal consequences?

He recalled how, back in the village, the Patils' daughter and the Kulkarnis' son were having a little rendezvous inside a thicket on the riverbank. Both were completely unaware of their surroundings. People were searching for them and calling out their names to no avail.

Back then, he'd fought off the other people who'd been on the prowl, and it was the same motivation with which he started moving towards Rafael, who, in turn, was approaching the woman whose arrival had almost caused three deaths. He intended to get his time's worth. The woman was flabbergasted at this sudden turn of events. The sight of these three bloodied men caused her to freeze and remain right where she was.

'There, it's them!' called out the young man who had accompanied her to the graveyard as he leapt out of the jeep. Upon hearing his voice, Rafael turned around, his eyes searching, before grabbing Girija – who was attempting to straighten her clothes – and planting a kiss on her lips. This was when Kashinath hit him with a stone, which hit his head. Rafael continued holding her against his chest with prodigious force before glancing behind him. The police had arrived, their batons aloft. When he saw one of the policemen rush towards them, gun in hand, he thirstily kissed Girija.

And then, a curtain of blood, issuing from his own head, obscured his vision entirely. He felt like he was truly, finally home. His hands limply fell to his sides. He looked at Kashinath and muttered, 'Kashinath…' and crumpled to the ground at Girija's feet. The sheer affection in his lips and the gentleness of his hands in his final moments was something Girija had never experienced. She felt irrationally connected to him. With a desire to cradle his head in her hands and stroke his hair, she was about to kneel, but then, the police shouted, 'Don't touch him!' She straightened and looked at Kashinath, her gaze smouldering.

जुलूम
Injustice

Frederick, a young carpenter, was overflowing with joy. He entered the slum with the disposition of a fragrant flower. He was ecstatic, thinking about the compliments a sahib had heaped upon his work. Perhaps that was why he hadn't noticed the changes in the slum. The usual crowd and chaos had been swallowed up, but he wasn't thinking about that. He was lost in a world of his own.

In this washed-out slum, his hamlet looked like a jewel sitting atop a trash heap. He didn't notice a dark cloud of fear hanging heavy over his house, nor did he think that it looked more decrepit than usual. He didn't even think it was strange that his wife, Eliza, wasn't waiting for him at the door with warmth in her eyes to welcome him.

He joyfully entered the house. Eliza, who would normally surge towards him like a wave lapping the shore during high tide, was sitting on the floor. Her face was clouded with anxiety. Frederick made an obvious judgement – maybe she'd witnessed a particularly violent fight in the slum and was frightened, or maybe it was her pregnancy that made her anxious? He pulled her close and asked, 'My beloved, aren't you feeling well today?'

His question, infused with love, made her choke. Her eyes welled up. Her soft, red lips quivered at the thought of answering him. She clung to him and started crying profusely.

'Don't be frightened. Pregnancy feels daunting, I know. Motherhood isn't easy. Okay, I'll make our bed, and then tell you all about today as we eat. Here, keep this…' He set down all of his day's earnings on the table and proceeded to make the bed. While shaking the mattress, he said, 'Eli, don't keep sitting. Keep the money in the cupboard, will you? And set the table for dinner. I'll finish up here.'

She got up and started fiddling around with the stove. He hummed to himself, thinking about the sequence of events that he wanted to narrate to her.

Only after he'd made the bed did he realize that he hadn't changed yet. The joyful tune didn't leave his lips as he changed and returned to the bed. His foot tapped to the same beat. His ecstatic behaviour made Eliza feel like her heart was going to burst.

This pure-hearted young man still didn't have the slightest doubt regarding Eliza's behaviour. Why was she so dejected? Why had she not greeted him when otherwise, she'd come to the door even if she was struck with fever? Why hadn't she insisted that he sit and eat before doing anything else? Why hadn't she counted the money like she usually did? None of these questions came to his mind. Instead, he was thinking about how he was hard at work for a sahib, staying on till the night to finish it up and how the sahib could not stop singing his praises. He was looking for the right words, the right expressions that would accurately convey these happy events, singing and tapping his foot to the tune of his own beat as he made their bed.

Eliza, who loved him beyond measure… Eliza, whose senses would get intoxicated at the sight of his bare body… Eliza, who noticed that he was looking unnaturally attractive today despite her mind being clouded with doubt. Eliza, who avoided looking at him despite all this could not stop herself from crying. The doubt and fear clawed at her mind and refused to diminish no matter what.

And then there was Freddy, who was buoyant with satisfaction. He did not know of the terrible incident that had taken place in front of their house and remained oblivious to his wife's state of mind. He had a habit of completely immersing himself in the task at hand – be it work or anything else – evident from the way he was fluffing up the pillows with rapt attention. He set her pillow down and exclaimed happily, 'Ellie, look at our lovely bed! And just look at your pillow; it's fully bloomed, like a rose…' She did not laugh as she usually would, given how he'd elevated this oil-stained pillow with his comparisons. Her heart quaked. A fearful voice echoed in her mind, 'My beloved, you won't even be able to sleep in peace on this bed you've made…'

'Nothing to say? And you haven't even set the table… Tell me, what's happened to you?'

Upon hearing this question, she took great pains to lace her voice with happiness and said, 'Every creation of yours is beautiful. The Lord has crafted your hands with great love. Your mind has been adorned with ambrosia.' Her heart swelled with grief as she uttered these words, so she turned around and wondered how she would wipe the tears that threatened to pour forth. At a loss, she absent-mindedly set the table and started serving him food instead.

His wife's loving, honeyed compliments made him happy. In a burst of emotion, he responded, 'Ellie, you look exceptionally beautiful of late, as if bursting with nectar. Come to me, won't you?'

She couldn't move, despite wanting to. She'd been hearing this sentence since she'd gotten pregnant. She liked hearing him describe her body with pleasure. But she couldn't think of a single line to get him in the mood. So, she put the food on the table and told him, 'Come, have dinner first. Maybe…' and she left without saying another word.

While he ate, she looked outside to see whether his enemy – Michael – had left anything behind. Then, she took stock of the wooden logs, hay and the cupboard containing his tools. She securely shut the door, and instead of sitting with him at the table, she stood before Jesus' photo and prayed to him, 'O God, please spare us. Help us escape this danger.' She kept repeating this one sentence over and over. Freddy finished eating, lit a cigarette and looked at her. She still wasn't done with her prayers. After a long while, she wiped her tear-stained face, but peace was nowhere to be found. He lay down on the bed. Her fears couldn't be quelled. Maybe Freddy's touch would help, she thought as she undressed and slipped into bed with him, hugging him tightly.

He chuckled and said, 'Well, thank you for this. But why haven't you eaten? A pregnant woman shouldn't starve herself, don't you know?'

A fresh wave of fear washed over her upon hearing that. Her chest tightened, and she decided to tell Freddy about the danger that was to come. Her voice was solemn. 'Freddy, in the afternoon today…'

He kissed her to lessen her fearfulness. She distanced herself from him and said, 'Look, just run away from here, right now.'

Now this wasn't anything new. She kept warning him like this whenever there was a fight in the slum, thinking that he might get involved. So, he told her, 'Not now, my dear…'

She was at a loss. How could she convey what she wanted to say? She turned around and started thinking.

Today, there were some blood spatters in their yard. The blood belonged to a gangster named Sakharam. Michael was a man with an extremely devious mind. He was someone who'd bear a grudge for years on end, and there was no telling what would cause him to swear vengeance against another. He'd made a lot of money by destroying supply wagons and selling alcohol illegally. The slum dwellers feared him. The police were in his pocket, too. His desire for her had caused a long-drawn enmity to take root between him and Freddy, and like the god of death, he'd often hatch all kinds of schemes to torment them. 'I'll end you', he'd tell Freddy whenever they fought, and he was her persistent source of sorrow. Now, Freddy would definitely be framed for this gangster's murder – this was the only thought running through her mind.

Again, fear gripped her, and a prayer left her lips, 'God, please have mercy on us. Deliver us from this evil.'

When he heard her plaintive prayer, he slid close to her and softly asked, 'Ellie, why are you so distressed? Did Michael threaten to kill me, or did he say he'd kidnap you? What is it? Please, tell me.'

The intensity, helplessness and sorrow embedded within that loaded question did not help her state of mind. She steadied herself, drying her tears, and said, 'Nothing like that.'

'Then what happened?' came his exasperated question. This man, who took care of his family through hard, honest work quivered internally because of Michael's terror, aware now that there was something bad that was coming his way.

'Murder!'

'Whose?'

'Sakharam's!'

'Sakharam's…? Oh God, what's going to happen now?' He fell silent after this. His strong, loving hands separated from her body. His ecstatic mind fell into a state of despair, and at that moment, a harsh light fell on their shanty. He angrily got up and yelled, 'Who is it?'

His jump startled her, and she tumbled to the side, naked. Then, grabbing a cover, she asked, 'Darling, what happened?'

Freddy just nodded 'nothing' like a mute. She fought to contain the uneasiness that was threatening to spill out of her, telling him, 'Freddy, take it easy. Remember, that in this world full of fiends, I have no one else but you.'

He didn't reassure her with his words or attempt to calm her down with his touch but simply lay there passively. After a while, when he heard footsteps near their door, he asked, 'Ellie, how did this happen? Where was he murdered?'

'Around three in the day. In our yard…'

'Our yard!' This was all he said before reverting into a still, corpse-like state. When she heard footsteps getting close, she fell on top of him and continued to sob, her face buried in his chest. Her grip on his body tightened, fearing that the police would come and take him.

And outside, a pack of dogs snarled and barked. The footsteps seemed to have stopped somewhere around their hut, and someone shoved the door. She started howling, 'Freddy… Freddy…'

'Why are you yelling?' he asked before hitting her above her chest. Her voice instantly dissipated, like ripples in a pool of still water. *Did my pregnant Eliza die?* This sudden fear caused him to get up, open the door and stumble outside. A rod instantly smashed the back of his head. A rifle pointed at his chest, and a pistol jabbed into his sides. Before he knew it, his artistic hands, so skilled at carving wood, were restrained and cuffed.

'Search it!' Police Inspector Pereira commanded. Freddy shook violently and stumbled, trying to get inside the house but was assailed by a hail of baton strikes. Still, he persisted because he knew that Eliza lay inside, completely naked.

'You scoundrel… trying to hide the knife you hid in the table after committing murder, eh? I am Pereira!' And instead of convincing Pereira that he wasn't the murderer, Freddy kept calling out to Eliza, saying, 'Eliza, cover yourself!'

But she didn't hear him because she had fallen unconscious, and the gazes of those searching the house roved over every inch of her body. Freddy's anger skyrocketed with every passing second. He wanted to get inside at any cost, telling Pereira to cover her with a blanket. But no one listened. Instead, every spring of his step was met with a sound thrashing.

The innocent Freddy was beaten, and the search of his premises continued. Michael and his goons were watching these events gleefully. The howling outside, coupled with all the slamming and other noises inside, caused Eliza to come to her senses. She'd barely managed to cover herself with the blanket near her foot before Pereira admonished her, 'You don't say a single word! It'll be your turn soon!'

It'll be your turn soon. These words painted a horrific, tragedy-wrought picture before her eyes. The heinous acts that would be committed against her when in custody, the shame – she could see all of it. The endless torrent of assault would eventually cause the child inside her to shrivel up and die. As she tormented herself with these visions, the car engine outside sprang to life. That sound swallowed up her visions and she cried, 'Freddy!'

The entirety of the slum shivered at the sound of her bloodcurdling scream. But the fear that Michael had instilled ensured that no one came out to try and comfort her.

When the fire in her heart subsided after her incessant crying, she approached Jesus' idol and prayed for help. Confident that God would indeed help her, she started sorting through clothes before choosing a set. Then, she took whatever money she could find inside the cupboard, locked the room and stepped out. She armed herself with a hockey stick to keep Michael at bay.

The police had left. She made her way through the chaotic, crowded slum, and reached a major road. A sudden thought crossed her mind – what if Michael framed her, too? It certainly didn't help to have the hockey stick in her hands, so she did away with her trusty weapon. As she walked, thoughts and memories of Freddy flooded her mind.

Like her, Frederick had grown up knowing only sorrow and poverty. She didn't have a father, and he didn't have a mother.

Her mother was a nanny, and his father, a skilled carpenter. He started gambling in a bid to get ahead in life, which hastened his spiral into a world of anxiety and alcoholism, eventually causing his death. Frederick, who'd learnt his father's trade, would take up any job to fill his stomach. After amassing some money, he rented a five-rupee, five-foot-wide shop on the road and jumped into the carpentry business by making and selling a variety of wooden goods. He also mended people's things and eventually started polishing and crafting furniture, too. One day, he visited a sahib's house, where Eliza worked as a housemaid, and was introduced to her. Their relationship deepened over time and transformed into love. A quick wedding later, she formally entered his hut, and their new life began.

Michael leched at her new, constantly evolving beauty and was besotted with her, pursuing her restlessly. He would say all kinds of things in Freddy's presence. Frustrated by his actions, Freddy often lodged formal complaints with the police, but they were all in Michael's pocket. One day, an exasperated Freddy attacked Michael and gave him a sound thrashing. After that, for the last five years, Michael had hounded Freddy. Today, he'd finally actualized the words he'd threatened them with: 'I will end you.' He'd finally pushed Freddy into a world of pain.

She rubbed her eyes as she walked. She constantly kept looking behind her out of fear, and when the police station loomed into view, she turned quite pale.

Her inexperience with the workings of a police station was visible as she asked any and everybody the same question: 'Where is Freddy?'

Some of the policemen laughed at her innocence. Others gave her scornful excuses, seeing it as a perfect opportunity to loot her. When helpless people were constantly rebuked, driven away and heckled, they'd often do anything – including paying handsome amounts – for a solution. The police knew this very well, and her mistreatment continued. They were rude and refused to tell her anything.

Time passed by. A variety of people could be seen here. Most of them were crying, distressed, stunned into silence, mournful, and others looked like delirious animals. From her position on a bench, she could see that those with a khadi cap commanded a lot more respect. She was telling one of them, who seemed enticed by her beauty and her youth, 'I want to meet Freddy. They've put him in prison without any reason…' Her words were punctuated by tearful sobs. The government servants merely listened to her before escaping.

Now, completely irritated, she was reaching her limit. One of the policemen saw this and approached her with fake concern dripping from his voice. 'Why are you sitting like this? Do you want to meet the sahib?'

'Yes!' Words and tears spilt out of her, thinking that God had finally shown her a sliver of mercy. She narrated Fredrick's entire story, but her naiveté served to only irritate her listener. He suppressed it, telling her, 'Yes, I know. Let's talk money, then…'

Her insides knotted uneasily as she saw his barely suppressed irritation and curtness. 'Money?'

'Yes. I'll have to ask my superior to allow you to see Frederick. I'll need five rupees for that…'

After she gave him five rupees, he told her to wait while he went in, never to return. She waited for him with unbridled expectation in her eyes. This was the beginning of the torment through which they dragged her innocent, simple soul.

After losing her patience, she asked the policeman standing at the door, '*Havildar* sahib, the man who took five rupees from me, why hasn't he returned yet?'

'What man?' the cop at the door asked her, irritated. 'Don't you have any shame? Who went inside? Who did you give money to? And what am I, your witness?'

'Please, you were watching!'

'When? Hah! Come on, now get out of here. You'll try to coerce me inside this police station? I've seen thousands like you, understand?'

His wicked accusations made her cry. She didn't know what to say or what to do. As is a poor person's lot, she cried to reduce her sorrows, drenched her tiny kerchief and kept quiet.

Time passed by again. And once more, the urge to see Freddy toyed with her being. She flagged a fat, ugly man who was entering. 'Sahib…'

'Yes, memsahib?' Despite his looks, his words were soft and full of understanding, she thought. She removed one rupee from her purse and kept it in his palm, saying, 'Please inquire about my Freddy. Please tell him, Eliza is waiting for you…' She wheezed while saying this before the urge to sob took over her entire body and she burst into tears. But no one around her seemed to feel an ounce of pity.

He nimbly pocketed the coin and twirled his moustache, telling her, 'Ma'am, please don't cry. I'll ask and come back to you.' He returned soon and excitedly told her, '*Arrey*, ma'am, why are you still crying? He's been released!'

'Released?' she asked, trying to make herself presentable with her drenched kerchief.

'Yes!'

'Truth will never die. Jesus will never let the innocent perish.'

She got up. Straightened her frock. Ran her fingers through her hair and anxiously looked at the door. The clever villain abused her in his mind before showing her the way out.

As naïve as she was, she waited with all her luminous lifeforce shining from her expectant eyes, periodically getting up for a better view. But Frederick wasn't coming out, and as time elapsed, she was convinced that this man had duped her, too.

She rose and tried to re-enter the station, but the policeman at the door grabbed her arm and pulled her back, saying, 'Sit down!'

'Where is Freddy?'

'He left.'

'When?'

'A while ago.'

'Meaning?'

'I don't know!' This response elicited a fresh bout of tears. The sound of her howls angered the sahib. He raged at the policeman near the door, 'Who the hell is this, howling like someone's died, eh?'

'A woman, sahib.'

'Who is she?' This question angered her.

'A young Christian!'

'Send her in!' On hearing this command, she twisted her kerchief, draining it before dabbing her face again, blew her nose, cleared her throat and straightened her frock before demurely entering the office.

The sahib motioned for her to sit on the bench. Before she could utter a word, the telephone rang. He motioned for her to keep quiet before picking up the phone, asking, 'What is it?'

She stifled and swallowed her sobs to avoid aggravating the sahib.

'A fight? Where?'

'The slum on the mountain! The slum was torched?'

'All of it?'

'I see, I see…'

'Really?'

'Whose shanty was burned?' Eliza asked anxiously.

'Someone living near your house, it seems.' Tears welled up in her eyes, thinking that Michael had set her home and very existence on fire. Then, the sahib bellowed, 'Get up! Your husband won't be getting any bail. Murderers or those arrested on suspicion of murder don't get bail. Now get up. I have a lot of other work to do. Out!'

'But – but he didn't commit murder!'

'Tell that to the court. Sawant, take this woman away!'

She got up by herself, not wanting the policeman at the door to put his hands on her. She blamed herself for crying because, otherwise, the sahib wouldn't have got irritated and he'd have taken her to Freddy. She reached the same spot and sat down while blaming herself.

All kinds of people were entering and exiting the station.

After the crowd had thinned a little, she called out to the policeman at the door and said, 'It would've been better if I hadn't cried earlier. That's my fault. Now, I'm ready to fall at your feet. Please ask the sahib. Should I get the bail amount? My Freddy really didn't commit murder, sir!'

'You're right! You shouldn't have cried. Our sahib doesn't like people crying. And look, this is a police station. There are thousands of fake, crafty con women who come here and weep. But the law is the law. Now, you seem sincere, so let me ask you something.'

'Ask away!'

'We know that he didn't commit murder. It'll be good if he's bailed out before twelve. Otherwise, they'll beat him within an inch of his life till he confesses…'

'My Freddy would never lie!'

'Then, he'll be beaten. If you want to avoid that, get the bail money. Go!' She stood up with the intent of getting it immediately. 'Oh, and how much money are you getting? Or are you just going off randomly?' His words made her feel foolish.

'How much will it take to free my beloved?'

'I'll ask, but…'

With great affection, she removed one rupee from her hand and sweetly told him to quickly ask the sahib.

He went inside. She was trying to hear what he was saying, but to her horror, from another direction, she heard words like 'hockey stick' and 'bloodied' from the mouths of people who sounded like the corrupt inspector, Pereira and the villain himself, Michael. Her heart skipped a beat, and Pereira's words echoed in her ears: 'It's your turn next.'

The sight of the satanic Michael made her want to run. She was positive that Pereira would arrest her after Michael filled his ears with falsehood. To avoid being disgraced, she attempted to make a quick getaway, but her legs wouldn't carry her fast enough.

'Ay, woman, wait!' Under the impression that a policeman had come to apprehend her, she got ready to run. But her legs had turned to stone, become one with the concrete below her. All she could do was quiver like a leaf with her back turned.

The policeman stifled the urge to laugh at her fearful, pathetic behaviour and declared, 'Bail is set at five thousand rupees!'

Upon hearing this from the policeman, she heaved a huge sigh of relief. She thanked God and started thinking about approaching every household she'd worked at for help regarding the payment. With this plan in mind, she hailed a taxi and sped off.

Back at the police station, a whip was assigned in the name of 'Frederick John Carpenter' with a loud announcement. The space was filled with a cruel tension. Now, the guilty and the innocent would all be put through the same grinder.

'You'll get the whip now!' said one of the policemen accompanying Frederick.

'But why? Despite my not having done anything? I have all kinds of proof that points to me being innocent, so why hit me? This is injustice!'

'You'd better confess quickly, Frederick. Then, there won't be any violence.' He pointed at one of the other squirming criminals.

'But I haven't murdered anyone, so why should I lie?' Another call for Frederick echoed in the premises while he was talking.

'You may not have, but why do you want to get hit? And if you want to withstand the pain, then drink some of your own piss.'

'*Chee! Chee!*' He stepped out of the cell with the courage of someone innocent, someone who believed that nothing would happen to them, that their testimony would be heard fairly.

An entire cohort of men wanting to thrash him thoroughly waited on the other side in a menacing circle. The sight of this herculean, strong, fearless youth with his innocent yet brave gait angered them no end, and they made a cruel, solemn vow to utterly break him down.

'Frederick, who committed this murder?' Pereira asked while stroking the whip.

'I didn't, sahib. I swear on Jesus Christ himself that I didn't do it. Michael might have done it because he's always had an eye on my wife. He harassed her in my presence, and one day, I put him in his place. Since then, for the last five years or so, he's been scheming and trying all kinds of things to get his revenge. He's the one who's framed me for this…'

There were tears in Frederick's eyes. He was eager to narrate a litany of Michael's misdeeds.

'Did you hit Michael?'

'Yes. How much could I endure?'

'So, it seems that you're quite the heartless one. You must've committed murder after all!'

'Not me!'

Pereira's fleshy hand, engorged with all the bribes he was accustomed to taking, rose ominously. Simultaneously, the fiends around him tightened the circle and fell upon the hapless Freddy, raining blows on him from every possible direction. After a short while, the courageous young man collapsed to the floor.

'He's pretending, the bastard!' Pereira lashed out with a kick. One of them held him upright and resumed the torrent of beatings.

He bleated like cattle, 'I'm not a murderer! I'm not—' Having partaken of Michael's money, his assailants did not listen to a word.

Knowing that screaming was an equally, if not more violent tactic, one of them yelled, 'You rascal, my hands are aching but not an honest word out of you, huh? You must've definitely committed murder!' And blind injustice kept raining down upon him. If he screamed, they would simply heckle him before resuming the punishment.

The endless stream of beating, combined with the pain, made him collapse over and over. He pled to God for dear life. But his assailants refused to stop. They joked around amongst themselves, poisoning his mind with their words, destroying it slowly but surely. No one was spared – not even his wife, whose character they assailed with the vilest profanities. And if he responded to these provocations, then they'd gift him with another round of thrashing.

He wailed, screamed and endured it all like prey, but all he had to say was, 'I didn't do it!'

And Eliza looked far and wide to collect the bail money. She knocked on all the doors she knew, crying and calling out to the occupants inside. If someone happened to take a peek from the window, she'd immediately narrate her tale of woe and beg them for some money. But no one else shared her absolute faith. Many of them were convinced that a man from the slums could certainly commit murder, and so, they rejected her and repeated the same truth, 'Anyone who's arrested on the suspicion of committing murder doesn't get bail,' but she refused to budge.

She cursed everyone, calling them lying, wicked fraudsters and continued her efforts to free her innocent husband – eventually going mad in the process…

तहान
Thirst

Those who couldn't even build a hut – the homeless, the street fiends, the hawkers – took refuge in the abandoned municipal school building at night. Amidst them, Doctor Bapu, Elder Dhondi, Punja Maharaj and Chindhya were the prominent ones. Usually, they'd occupy a corner, and they shared a rather harmonious relationship.

Four days ago, Doctor Bapu was caught by the police for hawking without legal permission. A lot of his goods were confiscated during this ordeal, and some goods were even destroyed. After his release, he went directly to Prof. Narayanrao Reddy, the man who would regularly supply him with medicines and tooth-cleansing powders, but the professor was unwilling to give him anything on credit. He tried his luck in a few other places but remained unsuccessful. This, coupled with another rather disturbing incident he'd experienced in jail, had made him despondent.

It was dusk. He arrived before the others and waited for Chindhya to show up. Among all of them, Chindhya was the only one with a steady livelihood. His employer was a generous man. He would give Chindhya one rupee and eight annas every day as pocket money, and occasionally, give him gifts that he liked. Chindhya also had a special relationship with his employer's beautiful daughter. On many occasions, he told Doctor Bapu that she'd give him money after he'd satiated her urges, which Doctor Bapu believed, because Chindhya was an especially loving, kind-hearted man. He'd helped him in the past. Punja used to harass Chindhya and goad him to no end, but Chindhya would never deny Punja because of their friendship. He was just that kind of a person. Charitable, good. And so, Doctor Bapu waited for his appearance as if he were a deity because he needed his help urgently. That incident during his time in custody made him feel revolted. Made him feel inferior, weak. He'd repeatedly entertained thoughts of suicide, too. He didn't want to be associated with this body, this life. Sometimes, he also thought about getting himself arrested and showing all those goons their place. In his imagination, he'd tear through them mercilessly. His disgust for them was unmatched.

Naturally, these thoughts that invoked sadness, loathing, revenge and frustration made him restless. He didn't want to feel it anymore, but that seemed impossible without Chindhya's help. Chindhya was a man of limitless compassion, gifted with the ability to enthral people with the power of his imagination, his words. He would've directly gone to where Chindhya worked, but despite asking him many times, Chindhya hadn't given him the exact address. He'd also given the Doctor a few satisfactory explanations for this secrecy, saying that his employer would be displeased and even fire him if random people showed up there. Chindhya confessed that he himself would feel conflicted if the Doctor came there and happened to stare at the employer's daughter. Their friendship would definitely be tested. Even if there were a threat to their lives, no one should come looking for him there.

This was why the Doctor declined when Elder Dhondi and Punja Maharaj offered to take him. He was also aware of how they were really gunning for Chindhya. Elder Dhondi, in particular, troubled Chindhya a lot, often hurling abuses at him, and Punja Maharaj always looked for opportunities to make Chindhya look like a fool, making the Doctor dislike them both. Elder Dhondi was built like the black precipice on the side of a perilous mountain – tall and imposing. His thick lips hung low, and his large, bull-like eyes were always tinctured red with the haze of marijuana. Whenever he spoke, it felt like someone was throwing boulders at your head. Punja Maharaj, on the other hand, was slender and short. The difference between him and Elder Dhondi was that of a goat standing before a massive hill. He was an exceptionally selfish, greedy and sneaky man. He was always perched around like a crow ready to strike and made a living by begging for alms. He was no friend to anyone – in need or deed. Then there was Elder Dhondi – always quick to anger, regardless of whether someone laughed heartily or cried their eyes out, or even spoke fondly about their wife and children. If someone sang a hymn to the gods, he would menacingly ask where their god was. If they said, 'He exists,' he'd sneer and retort with 'where' and 'show me'. If there was no forthcoming answer, he'd follow up with, 'If he isn't there then why take his name?' before concluding with his usual stream of abuses.

He would often narrate his own tale. His first wife ran away a fortnight after their wedding. After a month or two of his next marriage, the second wife attempted to take his life by poisoning him. He killed her by bludgeoning her with a pestle and did time for it. His mind was permanently warped by the time he was let go. He abhorred laughter, crying, the gods, and especially, women. When ticked off, he'd say things like, 'I'll smash your head in with a rock,' and no one took this to be an idle threat – everyone was fearful of what he might do.

And then there was Chindhya. He was young, tall and ectomorphic like a lean, supple stick. He laughed heartily when happy and was quick to tears when sadness struck. He was also peculiarly knowledgeable about women and their affairs, often narrating all kinds of indecent, lusty stories. He'd even tell them beautiful love stories on demand and had a seemingly endless supply of them. So, like a parched man thirsting for water, Doctor Bapu eagerly waited for Chindhya to arrive and infect him with his energy, to soothe his soul with his voice and help him rediscover the emotions of anger, enthusiasm and manly spirit that had disappeared from his own words. The slightest sound made him open his eyes eagerly, only to be disappointed that he hadn't arrived yet.

It was evening, and he was still waiting. The pensive darkness glumly stepped into the building, turning it pitch-black. Its occupants arrived, one by one, and spread their belongings on the floor before taking a seat. The Doctor was tired and distressed by the long wait because Chindhya was nowhere to be seen, but this was nothing new, because he didn't have any consistent or specific timings. Sleep overcame him. His tired neck sagged low. He hugged his knees and fell asleep. This was his favoured pose since childhood when overcome by sadness.

His father had died when he was rather young. He endured the pain that's often endured by orphaned children right up until the sixth grade, which was when his mother made a fatally wrong decision. This proud woman, who'd lived a life plagued by pain and sorrow, got pregnant and left her son to fend for himself. He didn't know where she went. From then on, he grew up eating the bitter pill called reality, picked up several languages because of the different kinds of people he lived with and became a force more potent than the aforementioned Prof. Narayanrao Reddy.

A few days ago, Doctor Bapu was standing before a textile mill to peddle his medicines. The crowd was transfixed by his enticing language, his fair skin, his innocent and delicate face. Their trust in him was assured. They complimented his rich Marathi, his resonant Hindi, and occasionally, his putrid, unpleasant-smelling medicine. Every now and then, he'd pick up a weighty tome from his collection and mention Caraka, Jivan and a few Arabian philosophers. He listed the merits of natural remedies while denouncing injections and pills. Made light of doctors and their profession. He'd warmed up the crowd rather well, but suddenly, the police vehicle – specially allocated for hawkers peddling their wares without permission – appeared. Many of them ran off with their wares in tow, indicating the presence of danger to their brethren. The desire to flee briefly occupied his mind, but he was rather pleased with the crowd he'd whipped up. So, he chose to keep talking to them, shoving his wares in their hands while demanding money in the same breath. Inevitably, the police arrived and threw him into their vehicle – wares and everything. His beloved customers didn't even bother paying before making themselves scarce.

As luck would have it, the police had also picked up some thugs and shoved them into the same holding cell that he was to occupy. The moment he was ushered in, these unsavoury elements eyed him from top to bottom, taking in his beautiful, soft features and his physique. One of them moved forward and quickly locked him in a tight embrace, saying, 'Come, come, darling, we've been holding it in for so long. Now quickly bend over, bend over…' And that lascivious thug applied pressure, trying to get him to bend. Another was trying to strip him of his pants, and a few others laughed with unmitigated glee. The rest of their troupe couldn't hold back and flew at him amidst a maelstrom of curses and crude ministrations. A few well-built goons were trying their best to throw him to the ground. He resisted them, vainly screaming for the police to come do something. As soon as he fell, one of the goons undid his pants. Another was naked before anybody could blink and started thrusting into his back. He screamed at these people who could not care less about another human being, having already lost their humanity.

This shameful, nightmarish memory venomously surged through his bloodstream, flooding every vein. His body shivered violently. Lips gnashed against one another in a fit of sheer rage, and like the spark from a flint, a word escaped from him, 'Murder!'

Elder Dhondi had been sitting in front of him – seemingly for a long time. The sight of the Doctor sleeping there like a child melted his hardened heart bit by bit, and he stroked him, his touch full of gentleness and warmth. For Dhondi, it was like experiencing the pleasure of touching a woman and the compassion one felt when embracing one's child, all in one. To be honest, he'd liked the Doctor ever since he'd become one of them. So enraptured had he been by the Doctor's mannerisms and looks, that he drew him close with the intent of being his friend – why, even a father figure! Dhondi respected him. And this was how the Doctor found himself being protected. Within a few days, everyone who arrived there respected him too – even more than they did Elder Dhondi, who, naturally, did not like this one bit. Despite that, he endured it without a word. Dhondi's patience finally ran out when the Doctor and Chindhya became close. Now, he'd often abuse him no end and look at Chindhya with pure loathing. And Chindhya, despite knowing Elder Dhondi's strength, did not seem to fear him at all! The Doctor would get quite incensed when Dhondi went off on his usual rants regarding women, love or sex – choosing to leave rather than listen to one more word. But he seemed to like what Chindhya had to say, and despite Elder Dhondi's vehement opposition, he had become rather close to him.

'What happened, Doctor? Who needs to be murdered? Me? Or the police? What happened?'

These husky words fell on his ears and awakened him. The sight of Dhondi looming over him like a storm cloud with his hand on his forehead and his covetous gaze, much like that of the thugs who had raped him – served to anger him beyond compare. And this wasn't the first time that this had happened. Elder Dhondi had had the same look in his eyes and had done pretty much the same thing as he lay asleep. The very thought made him snap. He angrily brushed off Elder Dhondi's hand, swore and stood up, ready to fight.

'I don't want anyone to touch me. The first fucker that tries it will bleed…' Elder Dhondi's love for him, which had been surging like water during high tide, receded swiftly at this response.

'Meanin'?' His voice was rough, a landslide kicking up a fusillade of dust and rubble. The tremors within it were enough to quell the Doctor's ire. Elder Dhondi sat, like a sack deflated and thrown to the ground, and mumbled inanely, his voice devoid of the prickliness it had earlier. 'Fuck, I… this world is no place for a decent person… You do right by someone, but then they turn on you instead. It kills me. I killed my wife by smashing her head with a boulder, by simply covering her mouth with my bare hands! And you dare abuse me, hmm?'

As Dhondi spoke, a pain blossomed deep inside him. He'd been feeling this every single day. Because of this, he couldn't even be angry at the Doctor (not with the intensity he wanted, anyway), nor could he forget how the Doctor had wronged him. The Doctor felt the same way. His heart had hardened beyond compare, twisted by the intense cruelty and anguish he'd had to endure in prison. The hand that had caressed him belonged to neither a father nor a man. If Chindhya showed up, he'd grab that chance to apologize to Dhondi – and lo and behold, he could hear footsteps. 'Elder sahib, I think Chindhya is here!' he yelled.

'Fuckin… that bloody arse fuck…' The incoming Punja heard Elder Dhondi's jagged abuse, saw the Doctor and cleansed his speech before letting it out, saying, 'And, my lord? Seems like you're displeased with your subjects?'

'And what gave it away, I grope someone's mother or something?'

This question sent shivers down Punja Maharaj and the Doctor's spines. The desire to smoke ganja while also alleviating Elder Dhondi's stress made Punja sit near him, muttering, 'Within the mind's bounds, bliss abounds.' He'd heard this line some three-four days ago, from a passing youth who was presumably humming a poem. Ever since the Doctor had taken to sleeping amidst them, Punja had developed a strange habit of collecting these random phrases and uttering them in all the wrong places.

Like the mouse appears tiny before the massive Ganapati, Punja was completely dwarfed by Elder Dhondi's frame. As the Doctor curiously looked on, waiting to see what kind of interaction these two would have, Chindhya announced his arrival, joyously yelling, 'Hellu, Doctor, Hellu, Elder, Hellu, Maharaj!'

'Come, come Chindhya, I've been waiting for you for a while now. Your employer – or perhaps, his elder daughter – didn't let you off early, is it?'

'Doctor, what to tell you? Today turned out to be a buttload of fun, I say…'

'*Arrey*, what is this fun? Come, come, tell me everything.'

'Look, look at this frivolous shit… like praising a fucking monkey, bloody hell…' Elder Dhondi hurled a salvo of abuses, and to get one over Chindhya, Punja added oil to the fire. 'You're right, Elder. Our minds may hold you in high esteem, but your mind belongs to the wild…' Realizing that he might have sounded too rustic, the shallow-minded Dhondi let it slide as he crushed the ganja in his hands. His anger wouldn't have subsided easily if he'd been sitting anywhere near Chindhya, who, in the sheer excitement of finally being in the Doctor's company, was babbling mindlessly.

'Doctor, what to tell you? Today was too much fun. As I was dusting the furniture at my employer's house, I entered his eldest daughter's room – yes, yes – and what a beautiful room it is! Soft, rosy, pink walls, the ceiling fan flapping about like a dove, the radio, table, chairs, a beautiful vase with flowers in it; she's got a nice, multi-hued sculpture of Radha–Krishna, blissfully lost in each other's embrace; a bed, adorned by a thick, feather-down mattress, covered by a bed sheet as white as a heron's wings on which lay a bra, and atop it all, was the lissom woman herself in a state of undress…' The trio was completely immersed in his vivid descriptions.

As soon as he stopped, Punja was the first to snap out of it, and to spite Chindhya, he lashed out. 'Yeah, yeah – it's the Elder here who's smoking ganja, but you're the one getting high instead, eh? Now give us a cigarette first and then bark all you want…' Elder Dhondi was in a forgiving mood (no doubt the ganja was at work), and Chindhya's urge to spit everything out was too strong, so he relented and removed his cigarette pack, accompanied by a lighter.

'What's that?' Chindhya had removed the lighter quite tactfully, knowing that the only way to shut Punja up would be to hand it over and sate his newfound curiosity. Feigning sadness, he mumbled, 'Lighter.'

'Let me see.'

He handed it over.

'Give it to me!'

'Fine, take it!'

'*Arrey*, your employer's given it to you. Use it for a few days, then give it to him,' the Doctor said, hearing the sadness in Chindhya's voice.

'Do you want it?' Punja asked, 'I'll never take anything that belongs to someone else.' To avoid any further bickering that would just prolong this entire affair, Chindhya hurriedly decided to end things. He wanted to keep going and tell them everything that was stirring inside him. 'Let it be, Doctor, my employer will give me another. Otherwise, I'll buy one myself… Money is no issue!'

'Ay, you fucking beggar spawn, talk properly! Be respectful, you hear?' Dhondi let another one fly.

'Forgive me, Doctor.' Chindhya responded fearfully, and this made the Doctor feel bad for him. Droplets of rage against Elder Dhondi and Punja Maharaj condensed in his mind, threatening to fall at any moment, and he was surprised at how scared Chindhya was of them. Seeing the Doctor's pensive face, Chindhya knew what was coming. He quickly deflected. 'She was naked…' He started describing his employer's daughter and her bare body. The Doctor excitedly laughed.

Elder Dhondi snapped at them instantly. 'Look, they've begun their wailing. A bloody mad house is what this is.'

Chindhya raised his voice to avoid any further interruptions and continued, 'She'd spread a cane mat on the floor. There was a rabbit-white pillow covering her waist, and she lay there, supine, with her legs spread out…'

He stopped purposefully, intending to resume his lurid descriptions with added excitement. His sharp mind was painting a rather lustful, long scenario, which he was busy envisaging while also thinking about the vivid descriptions that needed to accompany it. The Doctor's experiences with women were few and far between, if any. He was enthralled and excited beyond compare. He felt hot-blooded, his heartbeat was frenzied, his head was numbed by all the pounding and throbbing sounds within, and his body shivered involuntarily. His voice was laden with impatience and greed. 'Go on, tell us more…'

'Of course.' Chindhya described her glistening, lustrous neck, her breasts and lingered there, eventually reaching her navel. After these descriptions, his voice dried out, his mind foggy with desire. He was breathless. The Doctor, meanwhile, had reached the peak of his lust. His breathing was ragged. He was sweating all over. This cresting wave of sexual energy had submerged his newly puberty-struck, slick body, which couldn't possibly contain it. His lips trembled. All his senses were thrown into disarray, flickering like a lit candle wick in the gusting wind. He clawed at the wispy hair on his delicate face because his stubble pricked him on the inside of his mouth. He shifted his stance while sitting and slumped awkwardly. He stretched his arms and legs. He was overtaken by feverishness, and in the throes of lust, his hands unconsciously strayed all over his body. Elder Dhondi and Punja looked at his troubled state with pity. If this continued any longer, the Doctor would eventually be in Chindhya's thrall, and no longer associate with them. They were eagerly waiting for a chance to put Chindhya down.

And Chindhya was in the process of realizing the allure of the feminine form, that too, of a body he'd never even seen or experienced! The beauty of his own descriptions had intoxicated him. But his intoxication differed from the Doctor's. He was experiencing a higher, indifferent form of pleasure – the kind you experience when witnessing the splendour of nature. This indifference seeped into his behaviour. He fell silent and vacantly stared into the distance, and the Doctor's inner world, once replete with disgust, was now overflowing with virility. The abhorrent spectre of what he'd experienced in custody loomed over him no more… and fled. His imperfections and low points had all but disappeared, so he fearlessly said, 'Chindhya, go on… say something, my man…'

'What to say! I won't be able to say any more. What I saw cannot be described.'

'Huh? Now how does that happen?! One can always describe what one has seen!' The Doctor's voice had acquired an edge.

This edge sent Chindhya's panicked mind into a frenzy. He feared that his bare-faced lie would now be exposed. A doubt reared its head. *Has the Doctor figured it all out? No. If he'd caught on, he would surely hurl insults at me, like Dhondi.* This realization caused him no small measure of relief, followed by happiness at the thought of this educated, good-looking man being his friend, a friend who clung on to every word he'd said, and despite not having a clue about how to proceed, he continued, 'She raised her smooth, ivory-white legs…' And stopped again. The image of his wife, the Patil's daughter, and her scarred, leprosy-afflicted legs sprang to life in his head. He felt disgusted. In an attempt to stifle this feeling, he tried conjuring up an image of her before the disease – she was fair and beautiful again, as she used to be back when they lived in the village. Like a lotus blooms and emerges from the filth, he envisaged her comely form emerging from her now-decrepit body. Chindhya's imagination searched for the words to supplement these visions, but only chaos reigned supreme. By that point, the Doctor's thirst had consumed him. His erratic movements resembled those of a blind man in an unfamiliar environment, his limbs flapping about without any semblance of awareness or control. Dhondi couldn't help but pity the Doctor. He loathed Chindhya the way he would a man who enslaves and uses his own wife and daughter. Punja was peeved for other reasons: the Doctor was his mark, and Chindhya held too much sway over him now. With the intent of attempting to destroy Chindhya's formidable imagination, he barked, 'You pimp, fucking deadbeat, don't you dare pull the Doctor into the muck with you...' He quickly lowered his voice for the next bit because he knew the Doctor might get angry. 'That enchantress of your dreams must be beckoning you, eh, saying, "Come, piggy, come," isn't it?'

The Doctor happened to hear that and flared up. Now Punja and the Doctor were about to exchange some heated words and Chindhya feared the worst: his secret would finally be out. To avoid this, he shamelessly (and rather hastily) redirected the conversation with, 'My lord, she was exercising.'

Elder Dhondi had to acknowledge Chindhya's cunning nature at this point and begrudgingly considered that there was more to him after all. But despite that, he and Punja were all set to get up and catch him in the act. Chindhya was well aware, so he blithely continued, 'Of course, I bowed my head to avoid looking at her – her privacy was at stake, after all. But then she called out to me by the loving nickname she'd kept, saying, "Chindhu, bring me that towel, will you? And why are you bowing your head like a woman, dear?" Despite that, I didn't raise my head. I could see everything regardless. When I took a step towards her, she did a little dance and told me, "Chindhu, wipe my back now, will you?" Now that was like enduring a living death, I tell you...'

'Then?' The Doctor had gone beyond his limit. This one word incited Elder Dhondi. He selfishly wanted the Doctor to forever remain by his side so that they'd discuss books and other cultured ideas, and in turn, he'd improve his stature because of their enriching association. He jealously yelled, 'You demon spawn, shut your mouth, otherwise, I'll crush you under a bloody boulder, you hear? Shut. Your. Mouth!' The frustration made him retch after delivering this thunderous warning. His bloodshot eyes burned. Despite that, he glared at Chindhya with undisguised rage. He was ready to utterly destroy him if he continued these descriptions while hoping that he'd also retain the Doctor's friendship.

'Tell me!' The Doctor, having quite forgotten his encounter in jail, was aflame with desire.

'He won't tell you.' Elder Dhondi stifled a cough before responding.

'Why not?'

'Whatever he's saying is utter crap. All untrue!'

'It's completely true!'

'And how do you know that?' Punja's interjection wasn't welcomed by either of them. Chindhya was in deep thought, desperately looking for a way out of this situation.

'A lie can never be so vivid, so thrilling. He works there. And besides, these things are quite common in the houses of the rich!' the Doctor defended Chindhya.

'Have you seen any woman butt naked?' Dhondi retorted.

'No,' the Doctor admitted.

'Then why are you so sure?' Dhondi was persistent.

'Okay then, have you seen one?' he quickly retorted.

'Never fully naked, no.'

'Despite your age? All that experience?' The Doctor was incredulous.

'Yup. I've never seen one.'

'And why's that?'

'I don't go about ogling them. I don't like it,' Dhondi gruffly concluded.

'No, it's because it's obviously a lie!' Punja loudly inserted himself into the conversation again. The Doctor, convinced that he was just a selfish man with some sort of bone to pick with Chindhya, angrily yelled back, 'Oh, shut up! You're just jealous.'

'Watch your tongue, please.'

'And what'll you do if he doesn't, ha, you rat?' Elder Dhondi growled and whirled in Chindhya's direction, asking, 'Chindhya, is any of this true?'

Chindhya was stunned into silence. In the haze of his imagination, he'd definitely seen that mysterious, ethereal form. But the body didn't belong to his employer's daughter. If they said, 'show us', he was done for. Because his words were indeed just that – a lie. He was quiet. The Doctor snapped, 'Well, he's afraid of you both.'

'Why?'

'It's because he knows he's lying.'

'No!'

Just then, the sound of 'Kafeee!' could be heard. The coffee-wallah had announced his arrival. Punja Maharaj quickly exclaimed, 'Chindhya, come, buy us a coffee!'

'Coffee-wallah, here, please!' Praying fervently to the gods so that this situation could be averted, Chindhya sprang to his feet.

The angry Doctor yelled, 'No. Don't buy anybody any coffee.'

'Don't do that, Doctor. Let's not make it bigger than it is. Don't push me into despair.' He fell to the ground again, his hands and feet striking it like fallen logs. Then, he suddenly started sobbing rather loudly.

The sight of this young, dreamy, sensitive man who could be so affected by such a small conflict made the Doctor wish he'd taken back what he said. He was glad that he had such a compassionate, delicate heart. The respect he had for Chindhya increased a hundredfold. He tearfully relented. 'Fine, I won't make it bigger. Ask for the coffee, my friend; let it be served! Coffee-wallah! Let's drink coffee, count our blessings and have a good night's sleep. Call the coffee-wallah! Ay, coffee-wallah, come here!' He was holding back a mighty torrent of tears as he called out. This unfamiliar display of generosity and his tear-struck voice made Chindhya weary of the storm that was yet to come. The Doctor's obvious affection for Chindhya irritated the other two. Punja intended to loot Chindhya at any rate, so he, too, yelled, 'Ay, coffee-wallah, come here!'

Elder Dhondi remarked, 'Careful, lad. For a greedy man, even his tomb is too small.'

'But I can't help it! You'd have behaved like me too, Elder, if you'd had a wife or kids. In your case, it's "being alone, no sharing your throne"! Now look, my son is sick, and I need to send money to him, but I don't really have much.'

The Doctor, Elder Dhondi and Chindhya all knew that he was lying. Despite that, the Doctor asked, 'And how short are you?'

'Hmm, must be some fifty rupees short. Can't ask the Elder here. The Doctor's business just collapsed. Now let's see, we're at God's whim – whether he chooses to bless or curse us.'

The Doctor didn't want Chindhya to buckle and hand over the money just like that, so he immediately responded, 'Well, that's certainly true. Truth be told, even I'll need some twenty-odd rupees. Chindhya, see if your employer's ready to lend some? Ask him tomorrow, will you?'

'Nope, don't think he will. See, Doctor, I'd have handed you five rupees right now, but since Maharaj's son is ailing, I'll give him some. Let's wait a couple days and see what we can do for you.'

The Doctor was impressed at Chindhya's display of generosity. Elder Dhondi then said, 'Doctor, I'll give you the money.'

'No, please don't.'

'And why's that? Does my money sting like a scorpion?' Dhondi was miffed.

The Doctor hastily replied, 'Of course it doesn't, but—'

'But what? This bloody world, I tell you… why does no one think of me as their own…' Dhondi lamented.

'There you go again!'

'But isn't that the truth? Who's there for me? "Being alone, no sharing your throne" it seems. Just come with me tomorrow, will you?'

'Fine, I will!' The Doctor finally relented.

'Here's your coffee, brothers!' The coffee-wallah adjusted his lungi and sat down, saying, 'And, Chindhya sir? Keeping well?'

'All well, brother.'

'Take it, Elder!' the coffee-wallah said to Dhondi.

'I don't need freebies from anyone.'

'Oh, why are you saying that? Take it, Elder!' The Doctor's insistence was all it took for him to accept the cup. He quickly threw down a few swigs of the hot coffee but couldn't stomach it.

'Take it, Chindhya sir!' As the coffee-wallah was handing it over, the cup fell to the ground and shattered into pieces.

'*Arrey*, how did that happen now?' the coffee-wallah quipped.

'This sort of thing happens; sometimes things fall from my grasp,' Chindhya admitted.

'Why?!' the Doctor asked fearfully.

'It's leprosy,' said Dhondi.

'Heh! And how could he have gotten that?' Hoping for a diagnosis, the Doctor turned to Chindhya and asked, 'What's happening to you?'

'I don't feel sensation on my hands and feet. Don't realize it when something bites me. I can't feel anything when I pinch myself. People say it's XYZ. This is why I keep telling you to give me something for my hands and legs, but you don't listen—'

'Sounds like leprosy…' Dhondi struck again.

'No, no, it's just weakness.'

'Maybe, but the Doctor will be able to give us a better assessment. Maybe it's just weakness after all…' Punja cozied up to the Doctor in the hopes of getting those five rupees from Chindhya.

After having their coffee, the Doctor said, 'Now, off to bed. Shall we take the lord's name?'

Chindhya bellowed and invoked Rama, and Punja asked him, 'You're handing over the money, aren't you?'

'Here!' Chindhya gave him five rupees. Elder Dhondi made an exception and actually drank the coffee. The Doctor did not indulge in any further arguments. Chindhya was rather pleased with how all it took was five rupees to buy Punja Maharaj's silence, and he left their makeshift abode.

Punja Maharaj got up early the next day and went about his business. That left Doctor Bapu and Elder Dhondi, and the two of them emerged from the school building and went to a hotel. Elder Dhondi paid for their breakfast. They were standing in front of the hotel when suddenly, the Elder said, 'Well, what good is money to me? Here, take this – the twenty rupees you wanted. Now wait, let me just scout the area.'

After some time, he returned and said, 'Come with me!' The duo walked around for a while before reaching a chawl full of middle-class residents. Dhondi told him, 'Now wait here and see.'

After some time, who should they see but Punja Maharaj! And behind him was Chindhya, clad in extremely filthy clothing, leaning on a young, fair, but leprosy-afflicted woman for support as they took to the streets, begging for alms.

'See, that is your hard worker, and there, there goes the employer's comely daughter!'

The Doctor fell to the ground abruptly, like a tent when its central beam was pulled down.

'Chindhya, the Doctor is here...' Punja called out to him. Chindhya saw the Doctor and was utterly befuddled, and in his haste, he pushed the woman away from him. Frustrated, she yelled, 'You bastard, you came to me in the morning, kissed me, made love to me... said so many things – now come. Return to me at night and I'll show you, I swear, if I don't kick you in the fucking face...'

Chindhya was angered by the fact that she was humiliating him in the Doctor's presence.

'Hold your tongue, or you'll die by my hand...'

'Me? The daughter of Raja Patil, die by your hand?'

'Just keep your mouth shut. Don't shame me before the Doctor. I'd rather die!' He raised his voice, too.

'What doctor? What, him? So, it was for him that you were spending all that cash? Having all those baths and running about, wearing nice clothes to appear decent… for him? Is this the one you were fussing about, mothering, like a woman would, hmm?'

'It's over, Doctor, it's all over… If you would've murdered me yesterday, I'd have died a happy man. I toiled day and night to make sure you didn't think I was some beggarly lowlife. I even nurtured this wicked animal… And you're here… Now who do I go to, who do I talk to about what's on my mind?'

He started wailing loudly. His suffering whiplashed the Doctor into accepting reality, and with no small measure of anguish and frustration, he confronted Elder Dhondi. 'Why did you bring me here? Why did you rob me of my happiness?' In his frustration, he confronted the Elder.

'I wanted you.'

'You? Wanted me? For what?'

'I wanted to treat you, teach you and raise you like a son – and with this, open your eyes. You'd fallen prey to this beggar's wiles. I was enraged.'

'Here, keep it! Keep your money!'

'No, Doctor, don't do this. Don't leave us…' The boulder inside Elder Dhondi was melting, but the Doctor was furious. He flung the twenty rupees in the Elder's face, and Punja Maharaj began to shamelessly pick up the notes from the ground. The Doctor turned and walked away.

'Doctor!' Dhondi's voice was abrasive, booming, cavernous, a crag, cracking and separating from the mountainside and cascading to the ground.

'Doctor! Can I come with you?' Chindhya asked amidst all the tears.

The Doctor stopped and told him, 'Come, friend!' As soon as Elder Dhondi heard this, he could see nothing but red. His sledgehammer-like hands trembled with the urge to wring Chindhya's neck and kill the Doctor by slamming a boulder on his head.

'Don't you dare move! I'll end you if you so much as take a single step forward! Back the fuck off!' Elder Dhondi yelled at the advancing Chindhya.

'Where are you going, you rascal? Where is the love you had for me? The pure love you showed since we were children? And what, you think I'll let you go just like that, you idiot?!' Chindhya's wife caught him by the neck.

The Doctor, who had walked a fair distance away, turned around. Four pairs of eyes were sorrowfully looking into his. He stood and stared at them for a few moments, and finally, started walking back. Seeing him return, Chindhya, who was trying to get away from Patil's daughter, moved closer to her. She released her grip and pulled at the hem of the stole, veiling her face. Elder Dhondi's rage subsided, and Punja Maharaj vainly hunted for some words to suit the occasion. But all he could remember and mumble was, 'Within the mind's bounds, bliss abounds…'

कवितेचा जन्म

The Birth of a Poem

'Get out, you bloody beggar…' The haughty voice of his prospective employer still rang in his ears. The scorn embedded in those words was breaking open his proud soul bit by bit. He walked with his head hung low. The sahib's rotund, watermelon-esque face appeared on the ground, next to every step he took. His pace quickened with the desire to crush that face underfoot.

'You insulted me… me… me, don't you know who I am?' Voicing this out loud caused a thunderbolt to strike deep inside him. His blood boiled, and like birds are bound to frenziedly take off from a tempest-struck tormented tree, the words poured out from inside him:

'These hands of mine bound to balefire, will be as one with the sun;
but will return to the Earth – gripping the blazing sword of sin and rebirth…!'

His teeth gnashed against one another; his body straightened. At that very moment, the sahib's insult plunged into his heart like a rogue's dagger. He was fully immersed in his mind's turmoil, and after a few moments, the poison within metamorphosed into words.

'O Almighty… These hands that have cultivated love over aeons, where we find inscribed the history of a trailblazing culture; these hands within whom lie slumbering wonderous works of art… you've relinquished these hands into the maws of anguish, pure despair.'

The sight of these black, gaunt hands – which had risen impulsively, suddenly – tore his mind apart. It was reduced to an arid, blank state. He began praying for it to be flooded again in the hopes of experiencing the joy of fulfilment and looked skyward, trying to invoke an important memory – but to no avail. He couldn't seem to remember. His anxiety heightened. All that was left was the coarsely issued insult from the sahib's mouth, 'Get out, you bloody beggar…'

Melancholia assailed him. His back and neck ached. His limbs felt like they'd wilted and fallen. His empty stomach throbbed painfully… but what to do?

He stood, his back resting against a tree on the roadside, and it provided him with a moment of respite. That was before hot fumes began erupting from his nose and mouth.

Something had to be done. How could he return home empty-handed? He moved forward unconsciously, his body reinforcing that urge to do something. What to do? How could he get his hands on some money? He couldn't come up with anything. He was helpless, and this realization broke him down. His despondent mind spoke, *This country is but a boundless prison. I am an inmate here. And this life is but an extended punishment. But why am I the one being punished? What crime have I committed?*

Why should my luminous spirit occupy this black, pathetic, diminutive body? Or is it because my spirit, too, has been condemned to burn for eternity? No. My spirit cannot belong to a sinner. It is the culmination of a dream that's been dreamed for millennia. It is the narrator of an uplifting, transcendent life…

His inner confidence bloomed as soon as these sentences were uttered. He was now acutely experiencing the metaphysical greatness inherent within him. He remembered his merit manifesting itself shamelessly before others. He could taste satisfaction, manifesting on his tongue like honey. His gait was energetic now, spurred by the brilliance overflowing inside him. It quelled his hunger and tiredness. This intoxicating feeling amplified with time. His mind was overwhelmed; he couldn't see or hear anything at that point. A few moments went by like this. Then, suddenly, like an eagle swooping in from the horizon to perch on a mountaintop, something ethereal nestled inside his mind. Rejoicing, this inner voice spoke again. *And then, you were in heaven!* This line made him especially happy. He struggled to remain upright, and words flowed from him, a pristine stream issuing forth from rock.

And then, you were in heaven! You were proud of humankind, much like you are now. Your desires, your emotions spread far and wide, like the scent of a flower in bloom. The powers of the universe were pleased by you, your fragrance, bestowing upon you everything that you desired…

Once, on that very day, you sat in Indra's court. The gods herded sorrows and pains from all over the universe, coalesced into one. The many-armed Adharma whipped this essence of sorrow, saying, 'Salute Lord Indra! Salute the ascetics before you!'

Sorrow, desolate after having to leave heaven, saluted Indra and asked, 'O Lord, why have you exiled me from heaven? Where is it that you send me? Why?'

Indra ground the figure of man in the dirt and asked the writers of the sutras assembled there, 'O enlightened ones, what answer shall I give?'

And they responded as one, 'Bharat! India! Therein lies a land where shudras have made their home. Go there, live inside their houses, their minds, live there for the entirety of your existence!'

Upon realizing the terrible punishment being inflicted on these mud-born humans, you bellowed with the melody of the rain and the swiftness of thunder – Hell! The hell inside heaven, where sorrow still must be slain!

Upon listening to your eloquent speech, Indra-bound Pavan said, 'Beautiful!' The Pavan-bound Sea God exclaimed, 'Extremely beautiful!' And the Moon, bound to the Sea, mused, 'O Human, I will grant you happiness even during your sorrows. I will remain yours!'

The favour of the five elements angered the others: the armed Gods, Duty and the Sages. They assailed you with divine weapons and the scriptures, confined you and threw you to the ground. O brave, self-assured human, the selfishness of heaven is what made you a shudra!

The selfishness of heaven is what made you a shudra... This line resonated in his mind like a temple bell. The torches inside him burnt brightly. In their light, his greatness, which he'd otherwise been ignorant of, was illuminating him, setting fire to the pain and anguish inside him. He was convinced of it. This was why, despite his greatness, no one valued him – his mother, his wife would just not understand it. This made him revisit the fate that always befell him whenever he searched for a job...

It was his turn. The job opening was the usual: a daily labourer, but the company was from overseas, with good pay. He'd obtained written recommendations from two politicians to seal the deal. He'd even gauged the identity of the sahib who was hiring and switched from speaking English to fluent Gujarati. His flair for the language made the sahib sympathetically ask, 'Are you Gujarati?'

'No, I'm actually Marathi. But I have mastery over Gujarati, Hindi, Bengali and English.'

'Excellent, excellent, I think we shall be hiring you after all. You seem like a learned man.'

'What learned man? It's difficult to even exist here, sahib. So much so that the people in my household are but one step away from killing each other out of sheer frustration. Or take some sort of vengeance by committing suicide. That's why I get up at the crack of dawn and prostrate myself before the doors of several companies, one after another. Each day, I write at least ten job applications. Go to the employment exchange. The mind saddens. Life seems unbearable, so I head to the nearest library. Like a glutton, I consume those books on an empty stomach. I've studied all the isms – and just finished up with Marxism. *The Communist Manifesto* is beautiful, like poetry in prose, I thought. Great! I kept thinking about Khalil Gibran while reading it. Or about *The Prophet*...'

'Communist?' The sahib's demeanour changed.

'No, sahib, just some light reading!'

'Get out you... you bloody beggar!' the sahib shrieked.

'No, sahib, please don't do this. I'd have gone mad, had I not read it. I would've been burnt in the forest fire of life! Reading is all that keeps me going. Please, give me a job – any job! A sweeper, a peon – or if it pleases you, let me shine your shoes every day.'

In his desperation, he clung to the sahib's leg. Despite that, the pitiless sahib called the gatekeeper and threw him out after throwing in some painful blows.

Recalling this incident made him shiver with shame. His mind boiled with anger, sorrow and vengeance. Indignity weighed him down. He vainly tried escaping those thoughts, but instead, his anxiety kept increasing. His gait became erratic. The anguish inside his mind was leaving its mark on his face, assisted by the heat, sweat and dirt. He resembled an ailing man. Just then, a familiar voice fell upon his ears.

'*Jai Bheem*, master!' The secretary of the Slumdwellers Association stood before him, smiling, his hands joined together in a namaskar. He'd been quite the lowlife earlier. After accepting the poet as his guru, the man had imbibed a lot. Now, he toiled for the betterment of the slum, instilling progressive attitudes wherever he could. He was as straight as an arrow in a few days. 'Aren't you well?' the master asked worriedly. He could see that the man was plagued by something, and he didn't respond immediately.

The secretary continued, 'I was carrying all the necessary documentation and spoke to the commissioner in your words: "Sahib, earlier, your ancestors had confined us to a concentration camp and made prisoners of us all. Even today, you've built another camp in the slum." My words made the sahib sit up, alert. He regained some of his composure before asking, "Meaning?" I said, "You don't give us houses. You don't let us stay in the city. This impedes the development of the mind and the intellect. To live in the slum is to be worse off than a cave dweller. Sexual activity isn't confined to the bedroom but manifests itself before our parents, our young siblings and even our children. We give birth to the pillars of tomorrow inside all that filth, that cesspool. Murder, gambling, the illicit production of moonshine – this is what our children see growing up. How will the gods ever manifest in such an environment? How shall we grow and thrive? No, sahib, we've endured enough in the past. We cannot take it anymore. Now, people will rise. Once they're inflamed, who knows what they'll burn down…"'

'So then?' the master asked, barely containing his excitement.

'"I'll give you everything," said the commissioner. Made him give his word on it, starting with taps and toilets.'

'Very good!' said the master and continued walking. An empty stomach, coupled with a lot of incessant walking, ensured that he couldn't even stand. His desolation made it hard for him to share the secretary's enthusiasm. He couldn't appreciate the report, which was ever-increasing in length like Hanuman's tail. As he kept walking towards the slum, his journey was punctuated by novel experiences. The din of the crowd was getting louder. Almost everyone he saw was drunk. Venomous, crass and lusty conversation wafted into his ears. He was overcome by the urge to leave the slum for good. But his sadness was reaffirmed by the sombre realization that he was too poor to be dreaming about such things. He was sentenced to this life, condemned to be a prisoner. This truth was nothing but punishment. Despite his feelings, he entered the slum. His bewildered gaze took in the sight of people up in arms against each other, drunk beyond comprehension. There was nothing pleasing or soothing as far as the eye – or his mind – could see. The children had excreted wherever they could find some bare ground. Putrid pools of water gave off the most revolting stench possible. The nauseating hum of the mosquitoes and flies' wing beats could be heard as they swarmed around him. He was making his way through the slum like a sunray streaking through the darkness of hell when he heard Mallappa, the owner of the slum's illicit distillery, call out to him. '*Arrey*, oh, master! Get over here!'

He didn't like the tone of Mallappa's arrogant voice. But he turned anyway. Mallappa was sitting on his armchair, almost naked. He was listening to the radio, which was perched atop his pitch-black, flat-bottomed, pot-bellied stomach. His voice and frame made him look like he'd exceeded a thousand years of existence.

'How much is that for?' asked the teacher.

'Eight-hundred-and-a-half. Where were you?' Mallappa enquired.

'Got a job offer.'

'Get the job?'

'Nope.'

'Fuck me, why do you want a job anyway? Start a business. Talk to your sahib customers in English. Business safety guaranteed! Otherwise, come work for me. All you have to do is some accounting. I'll give you two hundred, cash. Food and drinks on the house – and that includes chicken and mutton by the way.'

Mallappa's words and his conceit tore into him like an enraged bear tears into their hapless prey, making him bleed profusely. However, he had no choice but to listen because he taught Mallappa's son English for ten rupees a month. Mallappa's business was roaring, too. He kept aside one hundred rupees to send his hooch via taxi, besides owning some three-four cars. His expert workers at the distillery drew a salary of ten rupees a day.

'Then, is it settled?'

'Mallappa seth, how can you ask me this? How can I work at an illegal distillery? What about my standards? What about my name?'

'Look, you've been roaming around for so many years now. Still no job. Now, if you'd chosen to run a business instead, you'd be sitting on thousands of rupees. Why are you afraid? The police are in my pocket. Take a look inside. Those senior officials are having their fill of food and drink. Want to eat? There's chicken.'

'No.'

'Your old woman lost her job today. And as hot-tempered as your hag is, she took it out on your wife – beat her till she bled, I tell you. Then, the public intervened and roughed up your mother…'

This news startled him. He began thinking about what could be done about this terrible situation at home. Mallappa continued, 'And what, there's bloody fights every day at your house! The old woman is always raging. Now tell me, won't our children end up learning abuses instead of any English, hmm?'

He was incensed beyond belief. To think that this uncultured, boorish, primitive alcohol peddler would point out his flaws! He lashed out instantly, 'Then don't send your son to me.'

'And what'll you eat? Stones?'

'Don't you worry about that. Don't send your son today.' He walked off angrily.

'This fuckin' master is his mother's spawn for sure. What a temper! Can't even take a joke.'

Mallappa's words reached his ears, and he reflected on them. Maybe his behaviour did befit a hot-tempered man after all. If Mallappa didn't send his son after this, then his family would be reduced to nothing. Not even a dog would feast on their carcass. There was really no need to be this arrogant. Maybe he should turn back and tell him to send his son over after all. But then again, to endure public slander from a man who drew his income from an illicit, shady business? His irritation returned, and he kept moving forward resolutely.

A crowd had amassed before his hut. Everyone was straining their heels and necks in an attempt to get a glimpse of what was happening inside. They were all too engrossed. His mother was cursing loudly. His wife's sister, Sakhu, was matching her, swear word for swear word. His heart was torn asunder listening to this vile cacophony. He didn't want to go home. Might as well turn back now. Reading something worthwhile at the library would still his mind. But the library was too far. And it was about to close. He moved forward, and Sakhu's voice struck his ears like an axe, 'You old hag, you tramp, shut your mouth, or I'll make sure your decrepit waist is dislocated – for good. Fucking gutter-whore, just after our lives like a leech…'

'May your mouth rot, may maggots infest it! May your tongue wilt and fall off. Don't get too haughty, you village-pleasing slut… Don't you dare provoke me.'

'Look, look at this – the dwarf spawn of a Brahmin… an image of a dutiful wife, eh? Sati-Savitri! Sita, eh… it's all because your son is a harmless cow. Otherwise, you'd have been kicked on your arse and thrown out of the house! What had my sister done, huh? I'm going to the police, and I'll fucking hand you over. Today, you broke open her head – tomorrow, you'll cut off her neck, you psychotic bitch!'

'I'll do it, too.'

'Do it, and then just see…'

Shaking with rage like a delirious man, he stepped forward and bellowed, 'Sakhu, hold your tongue.'

She fell silent as soon as she saw him and started weeping loudly. The sounds of her wailing enticed the crowd. They mercilessly abused the old woman with every filthy, vile word that they could think of at that point without any consideration whatsoever – not even the fact that he was right there. The old woman wasn't retreating either, cursing each one of them by name. He finally stopped at the door and addressed the throng.

'Go. All of you, just leave. As if it weren't enough… Now don't make a bigger scene, please.'

His eyes were laden with tears. His anguished voice made the crowd pity him. It thinned out, with them praising his disposition while abusing the old lady, then dissipated. His mother was undaunted, and hearing the crowd's receding insults, kept mumbling curses at him, his wife, and Sakhu and everyone else involved.

'Mother, what is wrong with you? Don't go around abusing everyone you see like you're possessed or something. If some psychopathic idiot gets provoked, then he'll kill you… and then me—'

'Good riddance. If you die, we'll be rid of this misfortune – an entire string of it!'

'So, you'll keep sullying your tongue. And eat other people's insults, too. Destroy what's left of your reputation and mine.'

'Yes!' She quickly grabbed the sickle lying beside her and gripped its handle tight. Her expression made it look like she was debating between two actions: eating him up or swallowing him whole. The red, murderous glint in her eyes made him shiver violently. He averted his gaze and looked at his wife, who lay on the floor groaning. He acutely felt her pain, his gaze laden with pity as it travelled over her form. The hem of her veil was caked with blood, and flies were already swarming over it. He couldn't help but feel compassion for her. As for his mother, there was only rage in his heart. Then, his gaze finally travelled to his teenage daughter, who was looking at him beseechingly. Her voice had turned hoarse from incessant crying. The emotions radiating from her eyes made his conscience crumble. She'd defecated right where she sat. The filth clung to her body. A swarm of flies had gathered over her, too.

Seeing the pain and distress in his eyes, the old woman flared up, 'You sissy, she's not dead yet! Not a single husband yet, and she's already putting on airs.'

He felt like the old woman was chewing into him like a ravenous animal, cracking his very bones. His rage was building up. But to avoid any further commotion, he kept his tone under control, saying, 'You don't want me to pick her up. Then why don't you do it instead? She's excreted here.'

'Throw some water on her arse for all I care! Or let the flies in!'

'*Aga*, why are you acting like a madwoman?'

'Who are you calling *aga*, you pimp?'

'*Aga* isn't an insult. Mother, why are you behaving like you've inhaled some ganja? How can you spew such vile abuse? What's with you, what's happened?'

'Ask this darling whore of yours. She's loosed a pack of snarling hounds on a rotting corpse… and she's your favourite, so you can't see her for what she is.' His patient tone was proving to be useless. The old woman was as fiery as ever and refused to budge. His irritation surged, and he said, 'And do I really need to ask her anything? The situation is quite clear. You hit her on the head with god knows what. She almost died. Don't do things like these; you'll commit murder!'

'You'll die, you bloody ape. Don't think she's some delicate flower. A wolf in sheep's clothing is what she is.'

'Just stop it. Don't tell me more.'

'And that whore with twelve bindis – at the house I work at – she asks for a banana while taking a shit and then follows it up with tea! The way she defecates… the way she looks at people… the way she eats. God! It's disgusting to the point where I'm scared! After experiencing this day after day, I finally told her, "No, I won't be coming into the bloody toilet to serve you!" She then starts abusing me. I gave it right back to her. Who the hell will put up with this every day? She roams around stark naked. Does whatever she pleases! And then, because I didn't listen to her, they kicked me out. When I asked for my money, the bitch refused – and then, had the gall to call the police! They took me to the station and only released me after some three-four hours. After all this, I was abusing that whore, but then, Sakhu thought I was abusing her instead! She tussled with me, hit me – look here…'

A fistful of hair had been uprooted from the old woman's head. The mangalsutra around her neck was broken. Her sari was torn. The cloth around her thighs was caked in mud.

'All of this happened at the behest of this… this harlot. So, I hit her. You want to take me somewhere? Take me to the fucking court! Jail is better than staying here. I don't want to eat anything that comes from her money… but then again, you don't feel for your mother. You want your wife. But what about your mother, hmm? She gets barked at by the daughter-in-law, those people in the streets and even her employer. Do you ask about that? I raised you. Gave you an education. Despite my brother's insistence, I wasted my youth looking after you. And why? Why? Have some shame…'

He couldn't listen anymore. He also couldn't fathom why the old woman had to keep scrutinizing the affairs between men and women, husbands and wives. She never spoke about anything else! His mind drew a blank. And the old woman thundered again, 'I'm losing my mind. The children are all but dead. Where is the sense in all this? You're at the library all day. And at night, you're tailing this vixen. Tuberculosis will take you. How will you get a job looking like a corpse? And when you die, she'll seek out another… Be careful… Stop doing what you do…'

'Ugh… what is this? Is this a mouth or a sewer?'

'Sewer? My mouth, a sewer? You lowlife, you fiend…' She'd reached the peak of her frustration and couldn't even pronounce her next words. Enraged, she swiped at him with the sickle. It cut into a vein in his leg. A stream of blood poured out. The sight of his blood made her gaze turn cold, unfeeling. The frustration on her face receded and was replaced by gloom.

And he was looking at her, too. The emptiness nesting within her eyes rendered him speechless. The old woman who forsook her own life to raise him was now out to kill him. Why? Did she turn into this person because of the physical and mental blows she'd endured? It had been months and months since he'd spoken to her properly, without reservations. She became bitter because he spent all his spare time conversing with his wife. For his mother, only cursory interactions remained. Did she keep assailing his manhood, his sex, because she wanted him to distance himself from his wife? And what was he supposed to do? Without his wife, what was even there? Who was there? Even if it was for a few fleeting moments, his wife was his medicine, his intoxication. She helped him forget the woes of the world. These thoughts overwhelmed him, and he was tear-struck. He swallowed all the rage he had for his mother and doused the fire inside his body. Mustering the affection he'd had for her in the past, he compassionately said, 'Mother! Please, forgive me!'

She heard his tender voice and immediately covered her face with a veil before hurrying outside. Her quivering heart threw out all her fiery emotions. 'My boy! *Arrey*, you are mine, bound to me by my seven divine vows! And I beat you? Tormented you like a demoness? I hit you…'

By the time she was at the door, tears were falling from her eyes.

'Wait! Wait, Mother, wait!' The ardent feelings in his heart were given form with these words.

And the strength in his utterances ensured that all their misunderstandings were tossed into the wind like tumbleweed in the desert. She howled with sheer grief and regret. 'I've only tormented my dutiful son… O God, smite me where I stand!' Her shrieking stirred his heart. So overwhelmed was he by this sudden wellspring of emotions that he picked up his daughter, exhausted from all the crying but still looking at him with a heart-piercing gaze emanating from within her innocent eyes, and his tenderness manifested through his arms, his eyes, as he gently caressed her in a bid to soothe her sorrows. He did not understand excreta. He wasn't disgusted. Her filth clung to his shirt, his wrist, and flies started to swarm there. But he was simply unaware. In his mind, a thick layer of storm clouds amassed… and all at once, lightning shot through the entirety of his being. 'Mother, these hands of yours… show them to sorrow. These hands that raised me, fed me – show them to sorrow. But when you return, bring death with you.'

He felt like something was amiss when these words exited his mouth. He wanted to end his adversity at any cost. He looked for some suitable words. But he could find none. All he could do was speak from his heart, coating his words with the spirit of sweet surrender…

He'd heard Lenin's prayer, which manifested into, 'Come, come O Death, terrible and extraordinarily beautiful Death, come! Death, come!'

His filth-stained daughter had fallen into a deep slumber, her head resting on his bony shoulder. He clenched her against his chest, eagerly waiting for Krishna to manifest within him. But that liminal, void-like, eternally changing shape inside was beyond observation and comprehension. In his struggle to capture it, he had lost his senses and sensibilities. He couldn't see anything, hear anything. His eyes overflowed with tears. He kept staring at the roof of his hut made of coconut branches. His mother had been standing in the doorway for an eternity, watching him. His wife had risen, too, her gaze fear struck. She thought, *This tender-hearted man, a man who counted the wings of passing butterflies, this husband of mine – has his mind crumbled because of our spat? Has he finally lost it?* His mother was weeping, too. She wanted to yell at the top of her voice and call out to him. But what if her voice, like a gunshot scatters the birds inside a serene forest, caused him to cast aside the child in his embrace and scatter, too? So, she stifled the voice trying to claw out of her throat, and amidst these gasps, kept looking at him. But he was unaware of it all. Line after line formed nascent in his mind…

…O Death!
You'll come, won't you?
Then arrive quickly
Before the heavenly bird of life escapes from the body's wish-fulfilling tree,
Come quickly, Death!
You'll come quickly, as planned –
Then, if your soft, tender hand
Touches my burning being,
It might end the momentary blaze that plagues my heart, unseeing
Strength shall be extinguished, age by age
And wounds, like old rivulets, shall fade to nothing, helping the pain assuage
Then, I shall be purified, good, youthful
Sometimes like Kabir, sometimes like Omar Khayyam

Who have gone but are immortalized by their depictions.
And then, swelling like a raincloud I shall soar in the air – sometimes
still, on mountaintops as I sing, my voice laid bare,
Illuminating songs –
Of my utterly beloved, magnificent death, songs of praise,
And of restoring the greatness that was wickedly snatched from you –
now and always!
Death, O Death… O Death…

He was full of haste now as he tried to find a piece of paper where he could actualize these words while juggling his daughter on his arm. He couldn't find it. His anxiety skyrocketed. To prevent himself from forgetting these words, he kept repeating them, murmuring under his breath, 'O Death, come quickly, O Death…'

Upon hearing him say this, his wife and mother both wailed loudly. His wife clung to him, periodically erupting like a volcano to ask, 'Why do you see things this way… death, death? Why talk about only death?! No, we won't fight anymore. I swear by your name, we will never fight again… Are you even listening?'

'My boy, don't fret over things like these… If I utter such vile words again, then I'll rip my own tongue out and hand it over to you… Look at me, my child. Look at your mother. My son borne of seven divine vows…' she bawled.

And he kept looking at them, his eyes full of tears at their sorrow.

Translator's Acknowledgements

I want to thank the people who were crucial to this process: my parents, for always being available to discuss the cumbersome translation process (and the status of Marathi literature at large); Shobha Bagul, for giving me the opportunity to translate this project when there's no dearth of translators clamouring to take up this task; Arshia Sattar, for being the invaluable mentor that most can only dream of. I must also thank Riya Matthew for catalysing the meeting which led to Arshia suggesting that I apply for the prestigious Yali Project in the first place. Thanks to Kanishka, my agent, for keeping in touch and dealing with the more troublesome aspects of the publishing process; to Sonali Jindal at Hachette for being the patient, meticulous and supportive editor that people like me cannot do without; to Hachette for seeing the potential in this book; to my fellows at the Yali Project – Ramaswamy, Volga and Sheena – for providing invaluable insights about the world of translation and publishing at large; and lastly, to the huge network of friends, family and people who have glanced through my work and provided something – from a simple shrug to a long tirade. You are all loved, and your time (which you'll never get back) is appreciated.

Baburao Bagul (1930–2008) was a Marathi writer, poet and playwright regarded as among the most prolific and influential Dalit voices of his generation. Born in Nashik and growing up in Mumbai, Bagul's oeuvre was shaped by Ambedkarite and Marxist thought, and he was a major figure in the radical group Dalit Panthers.

Manav Kambli is a writer, editor and translator with a degree in Literary and Cultural Studies from FLAME University, Pune. He has co-edited and contributed to *Jamshedpur: 100 Years and Counting* for The Marg Foundation and has published in literary magazines such as *Lila: Inter-Actions*, *Helter Skelter* and *Andolan*. Currently, his focus is on translating the works of marginalized Marathi authors, including Hamid Dalwai and Baburao Bagul.